Chaтом Coin Press

Charon Coin Press

STATE OF HORROR

ILLINOIS

-Edited by-
Jerry E. Benns

PO Box 478 High Ridge, Missouri 63049

Published by Charon Coin Press

Charon Coin Press
PO Box 478
High Ridge, MO 63049
www.charoncoinpress.com

Library of Congress Control Number: 2014949545
ISBN-13: 978-0692273760
ISBN-10: 069227376X

Printed in the United States of America

◊
Charon Coin Press
◊

"Where there is no imagination there is no horror."

Arthur Conan Doyle.

TABLE OF CONTENTS

Author Biographies

Charon Coin Press

ACKNOWLEDGMENTS

I want to start by thanking each of the authors who submitted to this anthology. I have enjoyed reading and being drawn in to your storytelling. I hope to read many more of your tales in the years to come. For those who are between the covers, thank you for the dedication to this project. Your efforts and words are what helped to bring this book all together.

I want to give a special thanks to my friend and series creator, Armand Rosamilia. It is your vision that began this journey. You have been there to lighten the mood and listen to me brainstorm—and then bring my grandiose plans back to reality. As much as I appreciate your support, I will never convert to worshiping your Red Sox. Not going to happen.

Laura W. gives me hope for the future of reading. She is a lover of books and a skilled proofreader—a talent she has lent to the benefit of this book and its readers. Thank you for your help and for being there when I needed you.

For all the late nights spent putting things together, editing, and working though the details of this book, one person was there to help review the edits, instruct me in the proper use of "that", and push me to the goal—Margie C. You have been a lifelong friend who has stuck around even when I have the tendency to pick on you. I cannot describe my appreciation for all you do.

To my children, thank you for supporting Dad while he was plugging away in his office. The four of you (that includes you TZ) help me stay balanced in my work and personal life. At the end of the day, you are the ones who matter. I hope I make you proud.

Christine, my wife, you have been there from the beginning of all this. You pick up the slack where I have been unable to do so. You have dealt with the many hours of brainstorming and lend your expertise to the process. I want to tell you I appreciate everything you do. Your support is what makes this possible, thank you.

Finally, I would like to thank the writing community for continuing to tell your stories for all of us to enjoy.

Jerry Benns

Chavin Coin Press

Charon Coin Press

INTRODUCTION

Why Illinois? I asked myself the same question while going through the selection process for the first unexplored state in the *State of Horror* series. Of all the states to choose, why would I want to begin with this specific one? I grew up in the border town of St. Louis, Missouri and leaving the comfortable surroundings of my known state was akin to going on an adventure to a strange new world. In reality, it was just crossing a river, and not an exciting crossing at all. However, for the younger me, those trips across the Mississippi River were some of the biggest adventures I embarked on as a child. As an adult, I have traveled the expanse of the state, soaking in the culture, history, and folklore. It is a state with its haunts, abandoned lake resorts, and history. The stories enclosed here sprouted into existence from the seeds of "what ifs" that are Illinois.

In the depth of winter, the fields lay barren and cold. The remnants of the recent harvest push through the layers of wind-driven snow. Not a soul would brave the bitter harshness, the northern winds scouring the remaining foliage from the fields. Highways and county roads cut paths across fields, running off into the distance towards small townships and the occasional solitary farms. Distant groves of trees sprout up in the fields, an indication of a house in the empty space. Hard to imagine this cold barren place is teeming with life during other times of the year. Summertime finds the farms as vast expanses of cultivated fields alive with towering stalks of corn and populated with hard-working dedicated souls. During the months of July and August, the heat, oppressive and heavy, rules this domain in stark contrast to the harsh desolation of winter.

Driving north on one of the many interstate highways,

one would leave the rolling hills adjoining the Kentucky border behind and travel into the river plains of the Midwest. To the west, lies the mighty Mississippi River and the expanse of the Great Plains. Continuing on our journey north, traversing through communities, which dot the landscape with their little houses, fenced yards, front porches, and streets laid out in perfect grids are the heart and souls of Middle America. The towns become larger and the fields give way to industry as the car moves further along the highway skirting the expanse of larger cities cropping up throughout the state. References to a president with his stovepipe hat cover the billboards, showing the state's pride in its past. Arriving at the final destination is the third most populated US city—Chicago a multi-cultural populace, bringing folklore, a rich history, and ideas from around the world into the very heart of the United States— the essence of Illinois clings to you with every mile.

In my travels throughout the country, Illinois has been the hub from which I must traverse to reach my destinations. With miles of open highways travelled, I have experienced where the imagination can explore. I was thrilled to see so many stories from different locales around Illinois. The authors did an amazing job of capturing the essence of all of Illinois to share with you.

In some ways, Illinois has always been a symbol of leaving on a great adventure. Join me as we cross over the border into The Land of Lincoln. Don't pay attention to the bloody handprint on the road sign…I am sure it means nothing.

Jerry E. Benns
Editor

Charon Coin Press

OUT COME THE WOLVES
by Claire C. Riley

I followed Artie—the red-bearded, army-camo-clad, wannabe leader of our little group—across the grass, traipsing over flowerbeds that had seen better days, with the sound of rapid gunfire reverberating in my ears. It was nonstop, and had been for several miles now. That's to be expected with a backdrop of the dead following in our wake.

Zombies, deaders, lurchers, walkers, whatever you want to call them, they've been chasing us down for miles—not the same ones, of course, but a constantly recruiting army of the dead.

"Get yo' ass moving, boy!" Artie yells at me, his lip pulled back into a crude snarl.

I pick up the pace and jog after him, my breath burning with every footstep. I'm not sure how much longer I can keep up this pace; unlike Artie and his crew, I'm not used to running long distances. I dodge around some trees, slide down a muddy embankment, and trip over a dark gray tombstone sticking up from the ground, almost as if it's mocking me. I stumble to one knee, gripping the cold concrete beneath my sweaty palm as the wind gushes from my lungs, my forehead bounces off the tombstone, then flies back hard enough to give me whiplash.

"Aaah," I gasp.

A fresh trickle of bleed weeps down my forehead and trails a path down my nose, where it drips into my mouth. I wince; stars—like in an old cartoon—begin circling above me. But I don't get to enjoy the pretty twinkles as a hand grips onto the crook of my elbow, and I squeeze my eyes closed and open in rapid succession as I look to see Lori.

"Get up—this is no time to rest, Numb-Nuts!" She holds a creamy colored hand out to me, and the contrast of my dark hand in hers seems almost perfect. She drags me to my feet and pulls me along with her. "Hurry the hell up, Michael!"

I'm still blinded by the blood running into my eyes and I swipe it away with the sleeve of my dirty green Antonio Pizza work shirt as we run—this time *not* running straight into any gravestones.

"Lori, Sydney, get over here." Artie yells again over a chorus of moans from the dead. "I've got an idea."

God, that man is always yelling. Never seems to matter who—me, Lori, zombies; he doesn't really seem to care so long as he gets to use that foghorn of a voice of his. I look to the left and see Sydney running alongside me, her knife in one hand and her gun in the other. She shakes her knife in the air, droplets of blood and gore flying in all directions. I cast my eyes behind me and see the dead still following, their group a little smaller than when they began their pursuit. Not that they care.

Zombies are like weeds: you take the head from one and another two grow in their place, as is the case in this situation. Even I can see the ground trembling in places, more dead climbing free from their wormy graves.

We reach Artie and he points to an overly large monument: Abraham Lincoln's final resting place. A grin spreads across his rugged face. The place is big, with two sets of wide, sweeping staircases going up either side of it to a viewing ledge at the top. The stark whiteness of the monument in the cemetery sends chills down my spine.

"We can't go in there, that's Abe's home," I gasp out. I suck in a mouthful of sour-tasting air as the zombies get closer. "Jesus," I grimace. "I can taste them." I spit next to me.

Lori dodges it and then slaps me upside the head. "Asshole." She scowls and wipes her hunting knife on the side of her pants. She's dark-haired, petite, and slightly chubby around the hips—or was possibly what you might call 'large' before the world went to hell and she starved off a couple of pounds. She looks at her knife again, making sure that it's both saliva and gore free. Damn thing is bigger than any knife I ever saw—black handled, serrated edge, and sharpened by hand to a deadly point.

Sydney is the other woman with us. She's crazy, tall, blonde, and lethal with a gun, but from what I've seen these past couple of days, she prefers hand-to-hand combat whenever she can. She carries twin silver-handled blades. She says that zombies don't wait in line and she likes to slice and dice them from both angles.

"You stay here then. That's where we're going, you little punk—at least until things quiet down." Artie nods to the women and keeps on running without a backward glance at me.

Artie has hated me since the first time he laid eyes on me. I have no idea what I've done to warrant such emotion from him. I prefer to think that it's nothing personal against me and that Artie was just hoping to repopulate the earth with his seedlings by keeping these fine young women as his concubines, but then I came along, and now there are two alpha males in his pack. I can understand that—after all, the world will need repopulating in time.

None of them are from around here, that much I know

for certain, but I've never had the courage to ask where they did come from.

Lori and Sydney take off, with a small gesture for me to follow, and I do, because—well, I don't have anywhere else to go. While these zombies are slow, they're also sneaky as hell and this trio of bad-assery is all I have right now. They're my family, friends, and protection. We have each other's backs through thick and thin. Well, as long as Artie understands the rules of the new world; he doesn't seem like a man who likes to share.

I jog after them, but as I come around a large tree, I see another problem: more meat-eaters surround the entrance. I only have my axe to protect me, and all things being said, it's a terrible weapon for an apocalypse. Damn thing gets stuck in heads too easily.

Artie is running straight into the mob of dead bodies, laughing like a coyote, with his knife swinging wildly; bodies are dropping around him at an alarming rate. He stops and whips out his gun again, a long-handled black and silver thing that he never lets me touch, and he begins firing into the masses of dead around him. The constant booming attracts the attention away from me and toward him, and gives me enough time to make it down the hill and head toward the main entrance of the tomb.

The girls have stopped to help him, fighting with some stray deads, but I jog up the three small steps and dodge around the bust of Abraham Lincoln's head, with his overly shiny nose—giving it a quick swipe with my hand for luck—and head straight toward the large wooden main door. I push it and miraculously it opens up. Inside is larger than I expected, and thankfully empty of anyone or anything else. I stand by the door, as one by one, my fellow fighters run inside. Lori is the last in, and together we slam it closed and latch it across.

I turn around and stare in amazement. "I was sure one of us was gonna croak it then." I laugh, my breath still coming out in short bursts. I stare around the circular room with a grin, happy to be alive, happy to have my little family with me.

"Are you being smart, boy?" Artie bites out, his small pink mouth moving between a mountain of gruff orange beard.

I shake my head no, surprised that again I've managed to piss this man off.

He stalks toward me, his brown beady eyes pinning me in place. I straighten my spine, ready to take it on the chin if I need to—God loves a fighter, but He respects a peacekeeper, thankfully Lori steps in and puts a hand on his chest just in time.

"I think he's slow. Just ignore him," she says and gives me an angry glare.

I'm not sure if she's talking about Artie or me—I'm assuming Artie, because I'm far from slow; in fact, I have an IQ of 130. I left school early, not because I couldn't hack it but because it bored me to tears; plus, the kids that went there were always total jerks to me. I hated being around the bad karma; those vibes stick to you like flies on bad meat—or so Pastor Gordon always said, and he was a man who talked a lot of sense. So I dropped out and got away from those people, but months later their words still hurt, even though I never saw them much anymore. Through this whole apocalypse, I never once prayed for their souls, and I know I should feel bad about that, but I don't. I look at Artie, all orange hair and anger issues, and wonder if I'm in any better position than I was then. Out of the lion's den, as they say…

After high school I couldn't get a job, despite intelligence. Eventually I stumbled upon Antonio's Pizza

Place by pure chance. The job sucked but I was earning some money, and money was the key to everything—or at least it was then. Now God has a different plan for us all.

Artie growls and stalks off to check out the security of the rest of this place. Sydney checks her pistol and then begins to reload it. I can't deny that it's hot the way she handles the weapon, each finger caressing each bullet as she slides it into place. She eyes me as she sticks the final bullet in. "What?" she snarls.

I shrug with a frown. "Nothing. Just looking." At the end of the world I'll easily pass up on Sydney's white-trash ass and her bad attitude for a side order of the lovely Lori. Besides, I'm sure Lori has a thing for me—why else would she always be so nice?

I pace around the room, examining the cold marble walls. I've never been here, which is ridiculous since this is where I grew up. Well, near here anyway. I previously lived over in Springfield just on the other side of Ninth Street. Mom bought one of those white-paneled bungalows for the sole purpose of making me a church-going boy like she always dreamed, and keeping my sorry ass out of jail like Dad. Our house was nearly right opposite the Illinois Department of Juvenile Justice. As if that wasn't enough, to get to my high school I had to ride my bike right past the Corrections Department. I shake my head at the memory. It was ridiculous to think that two buildings would deter me from a life of crime. I'm pretty sure that the red bricked Corrections Department was previously an old church, given its shape, which just made the irony of it all the more overwhelming. Besides, only God can save the man who wants to be saved.

◊ ◊ ◊ ◊

The hours tick by slowly, and while we thought the zombies would forget we were in here and wander off, they don't. The sounds coming through the wooden door indicate there must be hundreds of them now. Let's be honest: running into a cemetery wasn't the smartest move that Artie ever made, but I forgive him all the same. It's not like he did it on purpose. We'd been running down Monument Avenue, zombies coming from between those white-paneled houses on either side of the tree-lined road, and by the time we realized where the road led, it was too late to turn around.

Artie continues to pace the rooms, never settling for a moment, his eyes constantly watching me like a hawk, like I'm some sort of crazed maniac ready to pounce at any moment. I sigh and try to ignore it—ignore him as best I can. My mother always said, *'People gonna hate who they gonna hate. There ain't no rhyme or reason for people's prejudice, son.'* I don't like to think that she's right, but something about me irritates Artie. And while I'm not one to easily use the racism card, it's hard to ignore it when it's staring you in the face like an angry redneck. I rub my arms, feeling tired and worn down from all the running and all the struggling, but I have to keep upbeat, have to keep pushing forward, and trying. It may be the end of the world, but that's even more reason to make things work. Who knows how many people are left in the world? How many people may need *my* help?

"This place is huge," I mutter, more to myself than anyone else, since no one else is listening. I run a hand along the cool white marble walls. In the center of the room is Abe himself, sitting high up in his metal chair...or bronze, whatever it is—I was never very good at this sort of thing. I smile at him, giving him a small salute of gratitude, and then jump at the sound of more banging coming from the front door.

"Damn zombies." Sydney heads over to the door to double check their security. "Artie!" she hollers.

Artie comes out of a side corridor with Lori following closely behind. He passes me, giving me an obituary stare, and proceeds to the doorway. I can't help but wonder what they were doing down there all alone.

The three talk amongst themselves as the pounding from the other side of the door continues to grow. "What is it?" I ask, since no one is including me in the discussion. They continue to talk without even glancing in my direction. "Hello? Someone want to tell me what's going on? I'm part of this team too."

Artie turns around and scowls at me. "Look, you pimpled little shit, you are not—I repeat *not*—part of my team. You're just some little dipshit we picked up along the way that damn near got us all killed, and if I had my way I would have left you hiding out at that fucking high school. Now keep out of my way."

And with that he storms off in search of who knows what. Blood rushes to my cheeks. I'd be fuming if I wasn't so damn embarrassed. It's not my fault I have pimples—it's all the damn grease in the air at the pizza place.

Lori puts a hand on my arm. "Don't worry about it, I don't know what his problem is with you. None of this is your fault. I saw how you tried to save your classmates, how you tried to protect them. There wasn't anything else you could do. That's just how the chips fall sometimes." Her shoulders slump in sad resignation. "Look, the door isn't going to hold—at least we don't think so. There's too many of them out there." And as if for emphasis, the banging on the door steps up a notch. She quirks an eyebrow as if to say *told you so*, and I'm sure her mouth pulls up in a small smile. It does nothing to calm me down, but

I'm glad that I at least know what is going on now. Not that it's going to do me any good.

"For the record, Lanphier was my old high school. I don't go there anymore." I say with a huff, not wanting her to think I'm some high school boy; she needs to know I'm a man in this new world. I swallow my annoyance down and tell myself; I don't want to be *that* man. "Look, it's fine. He can be like that with me, that's okay." I shrug.

"He never struck me as that sort of man, picking on a kid." She looks puzzled.

"At the end of days, out come the wolves," I say with a shrug. "But again, I'm not a kid," I add on with emphasis.

She pouts and continues. "You seem the right age for high school, Michael, and that's where we found you. So if you weren't attending, then what were you doing there?"

"I was working when all this went down. I was delivering pizzas to some old school friends." I smile at the memory. "We hadn't seen each other in a while, but some people stick with you—some things you never forget."

"Oh, okay." She nods, her brow furrowing, but before she can say anything else, Artie shouts over to us.

"When you two bitches have finished playing happy families, if you could come and help us the fuck out, that'd be great." He heaves his large shoulders in annoyance.

Lori rolls her eyes and heads over, and I feel my anger bubbling to the surface again. I hate the way he says 'jump' and she says 'how high.' I follow her over, hands in my pockets and deep in thought.

"Hey, pencil-dick, you listening to this? I'm only saying this once." Spittle foams at the corner of his mouth, making me grimace. "I suggest that we stand either side of the doorway, one of us up high on Abe's lap over there, and when they come through those doors, we blast them back to hell." Artie laughs loudly, he seems a little manic as he tells us his genius plan, arms waving all over the place. "What the fuck are you staring at, boy?"

I realize that I've been gawking again. Damn, I hate it when I do that. The kids in Lanphier used to tease me all the time for that, calling me pervert and loony boy and stuff. I couldn't help it though; it's not a purposeful thing, I just get lost in my thoughts.

"I was just wondering what I'll be doing while you three are killing those things?" I shrug. "I'd like to help," I say calmly, not wanting to provoke him any further. Never provoke the beast.

Artie bursts out laughing, the sound echoing around the rotunda. "You will be tucked away safely in the coffin room, boy. Don't want you causing any more accidental deaths, do we?" His nostrils flare on his closing statement, his eyes scouring my face for something, a reaction of some sort.

I take a deep breath and nod sulkily, not wanting to provoke him any more. Artie turns back around and starts giving out orders. Lori begins scaling Abraham and Sydney heads over to one side of the door, both her weapons at the ready. Artie grabs my arm and drags me down one of the corridors. We come to another door that he opens and roughly shoves me inside.

"You stay in here, you little pissant. I don't want you fucking up this operation." He glares down at me.

He's much bigger than me at over six feet, with a head of untamed red hair and a matching beard. He wears army camo, but I'm not convinced that he was ever actually in the army—maybe a wannabe at some point in his life. His distaste for me is apparent, through his total lack of respect and the fact that he treats me like dirt from under his boot. Resentment and anger burn through me, but I keep in mind what my mom used to tell me. She'd say, '*Son, you can't change people if they don't want to be changed.'* She had a good point, but I always thought that Pastor Gordon over at Holy City Baptist Church had it right when he read one of his—and my—favorite scriptures: *And we know that all things work together for the good to them that love God, to them who are called according to His purpose.*

"I don't know why you hate me, Artie," I whisper to him, a sadness creeping into my voice, knowing that there's no redemption for him.

He splutters in anger. "I saw what you did back at Lanphier. There was no way that wasn't you who locked them all in there," he snarls his beard practically bristling in anger like the hairs on the back of a cat's neck.

"I don't know what you're talking about," I say dumbly and shrug for emphasis, but Artie isn't buying any of it.

"I saw you," he adds. "You were laughing and eating fucking pizza, watching them like they were a Saturday morning cartoon show." He narrows his beady little eyes at me. "I don't want you anywhere near my wife, so you're staying here until I know what the fuck to do with you."

"Your wife? Please, Lori doesn't even like you—and now God has other plans for her," I snap, my temper finally rising.

His eyes go wide, his face filling with red fury. "Lori doesn't even like *you*. She feels sorry for you is all. Now you stay away from her, you little pissant!"

I narrow my eyes. "She does not. She likes me, and I'm going to save us all."

He snorts in laughter. "You," he prods a fat finger into my chest, "are evil. You locked those poor kids in the room with the zombies. You were watching them getting eaten, all the while gorging yourself on pepperoni pizza!"

◊ ◊ ◊

Anger bubbles through me as I stare at Michael, the young African-American boy. He returns my stare with a coldness to match one of the dead outside. Something has been bugging me since we first picked him up, but it wasn't until today that I realized what.

That day a couple of weeks ago, me, my wife, and our next-door neighbor Sydney had been looking for a place to hole up. We'd been trapped inside an old McDonald's over on North Grand Avenue for days. Every time we'd tried to leave, hundreds of those damn zombies seemed to try to break in the door we were trying to leave from. The irony was, there was a history of heart attacks in my family, and for as far back as I could remember Lori had been on my case about being careful of what I ate. So I never ate fast food, always dodged Chinese restaurants and KFCs. It never really bothered me, but for some reason, I always wanted to eat at McDonald's. Now here I was at the end of the world, about to die inside one. I remember thinking to myself, *I guess those meaty patties everyone warned me away from got me in the end anyway.*

We decided that we either needed to accept we were going to die in there or get our asses out. It was crazy fucking Sydney who eventually came up with the bright idea of climbing up on to the damn roof. At least up there we could see in every direction. Besides, I couldn't stand being inside with all that rotting meat any longer—and I don't mean the zombies.

We managed to climb down and dodge between some small businesses and rundown homes. It was tough—the roads were so damn wide that it was no easy feat to get from one side to another without being spotted. We eventually realized we had been chasing our own tails, so we took a side road and ended up outside a couple of federal buildings.

Those places had rotting zombies banging at nearly every window, so we headed across the road to the high school. A couple of zombies managed to sniff us out but Sydney quickly diced them up, ending their short second lives quickly with knifepoints through the forehead. She used to be a chef, and her knife skills have come in handy these past weeks. We finally broke in through one of the higher windows of the building before any others found us. The place was eerily quiet, much like everywhere else these days, but something odd struck me inside that building: normally there was at least one or two of the dead shambling round, but there was…nothing. Five or ten minutes of stumbling around in the dark made it obvious why, at least to me.

The old gymnasium was locked up tight, heavy steel chains wrapped around the handles, and that's where the zombies were. We peered in through the small glass windows on the doors. Someone had been really clever and had trapped those dead fuckers inside. The others trailed off in search of who, but I spotted him first—Michael. As I stared through the window, looking across the gymnasium at the carnage and horror of mutilated bodies, I saw him, staring through the small window in the opposite door. The kid was stuffing pizza slices in his mouth and laughing as he watched the zombies eating his old school pals—like he was mimicking the zombies as he slid greasy slices in his greedy mouth. I pulled out my gun and went in search of him, ready to put an end to his fucking twistedness. But when we found him, the kid was crying and whimpering, no sign of the wicked person I had just seen, and I suddenly wasn't so sure of what I had just witnessed.

◊ ◊ ◊ ◊

A cracking sound echoes down the hallway, making me jump. Artie seems to like that.

"I saw you, boy. I saw you before you saw me," he snarls.

"Artie! They're coming!" Sydney yells out, just as the sound of the front door exploding open booms loudly.

Firing erupts, and the groans and moans of the dead awaken something in me. The noises sound twice as loud coming from the rotunda because of its shape and size.

"I don't trust you for a second. It took me a while, but now I know that I didn't imagine it—I know that was you eating pizza, with no remorse for the dead and their suffering."

I smile. "No remorse at all."

"You being fucking funny with me, boy?" He glares.

I shake my head no and smile wider. He turns to go back and help the girls, and I take this as my opportunity, stepping forward as I drive my axe into his back.

He calls out loudly and then falls to his knees, crying in pain as blood pumps around my axe and his hands grasp blindly behind him. I press my shoe into his back, and he sprawls forward with a thump.

"I showed no remorse, Artie, because I locked them in there. The new world doesn't need sinners, and they were sinners through and through: whores, drug users, and bullies. Most of them would have grown up to be nothing more than toilet paper for the world anyway." I yank the axe out of him before quickly smashing it into the base of his skull. Blood splatters up the walls as I pound into him again and again, turning his skull to crumbled eggshells. The smell of blood must attract the zombies, as they begin to trickle down the hallway toward us with reaching rotten arms. I step back inside the coffin room and close the door silently behind me.

The sounds of the dead feasting on Artie fill me with a profound sense of achievement. "I was called, and I responded to that call, Father. He who hast become the monster will destroy the monsters," I whisper into the circular room. I look up to the gold ceiling with a smile. Even here, God shines His light upon me, as if blessing me. "My calling came one day, when the dead did rise, when life turned to gore and grime, and those that were filled with hate and anger did burn to the ground, only to be reanimated into the emancipation of the devil himself. I shall destroy all that is evil. I shall destroy all that do harm."

I think on Artie's words that he saw me, and smile at the memory of my old dead classmates. They all got what they deserved. In life they were all horrible human beings, always teasing and tormenting, but I got the last laugh—because I was the one who trapped them in the room full of zombies, watching them be killed, and in turn, be changed into their worst nightmares.

I watched them for days, feasting on the rotting, graying flesh of their fellow students. I would have quite happily stayed there until all this blew over, until the government came to put an end to the world's suffering and protect the innocents left, but God had other plans for me.

He delivered Artie and his team, I rescued them, took them under my wing and let them stay at the school, but it was never enough for them—I was never enough for them. The only one that ever cared was Lori. I smile again and crack the door open.

I hope she's alive still. God has a calling for her, too; together we're going to repopulate the earth.

RITTER HOUSE
by A. Lopez, Jr.

"Shadows of deceased ghosts do haunt the houses and the graves about, whose life's lamp went untimely out."

"Test, test. I am going to record the next twelve hours or so, for my research project for my next novel, yet to be named. It is 5:30 p.m. Friday, July 22, 2011. I am horror author, Peter Keller. I am labeled as a horror author in the sense that I tend to write about such things, and in turn, it allows my fans and critics alike, to find a starting point to attach themselves to me and my style. I'm not big on labels, but in fairness to everyone, I do tend to dabble in the horror and macabre. I can't complain, and my next novel will be much enhanced by my visit to the famed and notorious, Ritter House. I am staying a night and making this recording in audio form and with pen and paper only. The owner and proprietor of the house, and a very kind gentleman if I may say, Daniel Ritter, asked that there be no video recordings done while I am inside. I had no issue with that and will respect his wishes. After all, I am going there for my research, to absorb the elements of the home and take in the true feel of the energy that is supposed to haunt the place. I am not a paranormal investigator or scientist in any form, as my wife can attest to. I am just a man who prefers to research the material that I will deliver to your mind's eye. My intention is to go in without any direct plan or agenda, other than to experience the house for what it is. And yes, I am aware of the history and things that have gone on there, and of what people have said they have experienced. I am not blind to that fact at all, but I do go in open-minded. I will go into the detail of the history of the house when I arrive there in an hour or so."

"It is now 7:00 p.m. and I have been let in the house by Mr. Ritter. I plan on staying here for twelve hours and take notes accordingly. I asked Mr. Ritter to shut down the electricity, but he insisted on leaving on the breaker that controls the first floor bathroom. As I think on it, I can't say I disagree. Running water will be available if I need. In my possession, I will have a flashlight, a digital audio recorder, a pad of paper and pen, a cell phone, for emergencies only mind you, and my laptop computer with an extra battery—I plan to write as the mood hits me. I have also brought a snack and water. I will make my next recording after nightfall draws on the old house."

"The night has spoken; it is now completely dark in the house. In the past two hours I have walked around the downstairs of the house so I could get my bearings. It is a nice house really, full of furniture and ready for someone to move right in. But, I believe that is easier said than done, as Ritter House has not had a tenant, according to Mr. Ritter, in ten years. I must say, he really keeps the place up quite well. The house is very clean and not dusty at all, although I am looking at all this through the light of my flashlight. I have set up shop, so to speak, in the living room at a rather nice desk. The desk is made of solid wood and as far as I can tell, no expense has been spared in the décor of this place. I'll take a seat there and go over my notes."

"A few notes about the Ritter House. It is located, as

most who follow haunted houses know, in a small neighborhood just south of Cicero, Illinois, not far from my home in suburban Chicago. The house is a three-bedroom, two-bath, two-story home. It was built in 1948 making it at least sixty-three years old, by my math. The house was built and was owned by Nicholas and Debra Blakely and that is why the house is sometimes referred to as Blakely House. The Blakely's were life-long residents of Illinois and in 1951 Debra Blakely had dinner with her husband, washed the dishes and walked outside to the backyard shed. She brought back with her an axe and hacksaw. As her husband Nicholas slept in his living room chair, she raised the axe above her, from behind him, and brought it down on his head. The axe slicing through his skull killed him instantly. After a couple of more blows he had fallen out of the chair to the floor. Thank God for him, he died on the first blow rather than endure his lovely wife taking the hacksaw and cutting him into six pieces; two legs, two arms, his torso and his head. Debra was found wandering the streets that night covered in blood, and in the state of mind of a lost soul. Her words were to no one in particular, but those words set the tone for the reputation and history of the house."

'The devil made me do it. The devil made me do it.' These were the words that Debra Blakely spoke when authorities questioned her. The pieces of Nicholas' bloody body were found that night, July 22, 1951, in the exact spot that I am sitting now. Debra committed suicide while in jail four months later with authorities never getting an explanation of why. Yes, tonight is the sixty year anniversary of the murder. Debra's claim was that the devil made her do it... noted. But, there is more to the story of Ritter House, it seems. First I must take a quick break."

"I guess I am getting old or tired. I went to the

bathroom and as I came out I thought I heard a door close down the hall. The doors to the two downstairs rooms were open, so I thought the sound could have been one of the closet doors. I walked to each room, and in the second room the closet door was closed. I do not scare easily, but I must admit with only my flashlight to guide me, the room did take on a dark, gloomy look. I reached for the door knob and turned. As I pulled the door open, I shined the light inside the closet. It was empty, with only a few hangers and a shelf looking back at me. I did smile over the little incident. I do not know what the sound was, but I can report that I found nothing."

"Now, I'll finish off what I know about the history of this house. The house remained vacant for three years after the Blakely murder, and rumors of the place being haunted by either the ghost of Nicholas Blakely or worse, by a demon, quickly spread through town until new owners were found. Let's see here, William and Mary Ritter bought the house for the low price of $8,000.00. Considering what had happened, I'm surprised they didn't just give it away. According to some of the *old-timers* around here, there were no odd or strange reports about the house after the Ritters moved in. That was until two years later in 1956. Again, according to reports, while the Ritter children were away with relatives, William Ritter took a shotgun and shot his wife Mary three times while she slept. It is agreed by investigators, he then walked into the hallway just outside their bedroom, where he turned the gun on himself. No one reported hearing any gunshots, probably due to the thunderstorms that night. From that time, the Ritter family has owned the house. The kind young man Daniel, who let me in and agreed to me being here, is the nephew of William and Mary. Apparently, no one has lived here for more than a month before they moved out, claiming this place to be haunted or possessed. Daniel has had ownership of the house since 1994. He hasn't changed much about the place. He doesn't even list it as rental property, and from what he says, he holds on to the place in memory of his family, despite the tragedy. I asked him if he had experienced anything paranormal here. He didn't answer me."

"The old pendulum clock on the wall, that I set the time on when I arrived, now says the time is midnight. I was pleasantly surprised it still worked. After taking a short break to write down some notes and write a little on the computer, I am ready to explore the upstairs thoroughly. Just as a side note, before I made my trek here, I looked up the history of the land before houses were built here. This part of south Cicero is riddled with old stories and legends of all kind, most undocumented. I could not find any information, through several resources, that there was anything unusual here, other than just a piece of land on a hill. I did talk to one older gentleman who said his father told him the land on the hill here was tainted, that it was cursed. He recalled his father telling him that long ago, before the houses, murdered bodies were buried here on the hill. His father forbade him from playing in this area. I have found no proof, nor have I heard of anything like that in my research. I'll grab my flashlight and head upstairs."

"I plan to look around further downstairs after I finish looking around upstairs. So far I have not encountered anything unusual, other than the sound of a door slamming. I carry with me, a flashlight, a digital audio recorder, and in my pocket, my cell phone, which my wife insisted I bring. The stairs are old and wooden and creak with each step I take. As I look around, again I notice, even with the limited view of my flashlight, the place is very well kept. There are pictures on the wall here as I ascend the stairs. No recent pictures, only older ones. Here is a picture of The Ritter family, William, Mary and kids. They are similar to the pictures I have seen of them in my research. It is very dark up here. The air is musty—that of old carpet. The upstairs is a bit smaller than below, and as I stand at the top of the stairs, to my left is a small office that I will venture in first."

"The office is the typical setup of a desk, a chair, and a lamp. A small bookshelf accompanies it on the west wall and a nice window view of the backyard makes me think this would be a nice place to write a novel. Of course that's the writer in me speaking there. I think I'll sit at the desk and soak in the atmosphere of the room for a moment."

"I have sat here for roughly ten minutes, concentrating and listening, trying to absorb the dark vibe that must associate this place, considering the murders which have taken place here. Sitting in a dark room and closing the eyes is the best way take in the hidden vibe of an evil place. In my warped way of thinking, it will help me later in my writing, when I recall the feelings or chills I might experience from a place like this. It's time to visit the scene of the murder-suicide."

"The hallway is lined with very nice wood paneling from one end to the other. I am at the doorway of the office, looking down the hallway. My flashlight is strong and the light is bearing down on the bathroom directly at the end of the hall. Knowing that William Ritter committed suicide in this hall, right outside the door of the adjacent bedroom, does give me a little pause before I walk down there. I don't see anything other than what is supposed to be there, but for the first time I do feel apprehensive. The hall is not long and I can see the light reflecting off of the mirror in the bathroom as I get closer."

"I am now standing in the spot where William ended

his life, just outside the bedroom and against the hallway wall. I feel a bit of a chill standing here I must admit. As I stated prior, I am not a paranormal investigator, and I do not relate chills or anything other than an actual visual experience, to anything more than what it is, but it is a bit colder here. As it is very dark in here I can see how many people, if put in this situation, could be scared and let their imagination run wild. This house is not the most uplifting place for a wayward soul. I am now shining the light into the bedroom of William and Mary. The bed is clearly visible from here. I can only imagine what was going through William's mind just before he ended his life. From this spot he could clearly see his wife's dead body and the blood-splattered white sheets. For me, it's unthinkable."

"Upon entering the bedroom, it appears the furnishings here are not modern, nor are they from the last two decades to be sure, and it is just as Daniel told me it would be. I am assuming this is how the room was that terrible, stormy night. The four-post bed is of beautiful construction. The wooden frame is stained in a dark, cherry wood. Looking around the room I can see that all of the furniture in here is a matching set with the bed, very nice indeed. The view from the window looks out over the front yard and street. This house has a slightly higher post than the others on the street as it sits at the highest point of a small hill. Not much stirring outside and not much stirring in here. I must check out the closet. Closets can tell a lot of a person, and I am curious as to the state of this one. The door creaked loudly, almost as if it was singing, or telling the story of what it witnessed that night. I like that line; I may just use it in my next novel. The closet is completely empty except for a white dress that hangs in the dark corner to the far right...strange. It looks as if it hasn't been disturbed in years, and I will not disturb it now. The closet door has a full-length mirror attached to it and as you close it, from this point of view, you can see the bed. I am sure that this mirror has its own story of the murder it witnessed as well."

The sound of the wooden floor creaking behind Peter causes him to be silent and listen. He turns quickly.

"I just heard a noise behind me, but nothing is there. The floor creaked as if someone was walking slowly across it. Maybe the wind or maybe, *my* imagination is running wild as have others here. Now I will go take a look around in the bathroom across the hall."

"The hall is quite cold, much colder than it should be. Maybe there is a draft coming in here from the attic. The bathroom is similar to the one downstairs except it is bigger and has an oval-shaped window. The bathroom is completely white, even the faucets and knobs for the drawers and cabinets are white. Someone definitely had an obsession with white."

"The only place I have not seen in this house is the attic. Mr. Ritter would not grant me access to it for safety concerns. I will head back downstairs only to return here at 2:45 a.m., the approximate time of the murder-suicide, when at that time, I will lie in Mary's bed."

As Peter is about to descend the stairs he hears a slow, thump…thump…thump, of what sounds like someone walking down the hall towards him. He shines the light down the hall quickly, the noise stops.

"I just thought I heard someone walking towards me in the hall here. No one is there, but I will replay this audio later to see if it picked up that sound. I am here to take in the feel of this house and so far, that has been the only thing to give me pause. What I just heard sounded very real to me."

He finally takes the light from the hall and shines it down the stairs so he can see as he makes his descent to the first floor.

"I am sitting back at the desk making notes. It is nearly one-in-the-morning, and I find myself very much awake. I will not play back any audio until tomorrow morning when I leave here and I am taking a break and reflecting on what I have experienced thus far. Practically nothing, but I can say I have been a little on edge a couple of times. This house has a terrible history and reputation as one of the most haunted houses in America, and no matter what has or hasn't happened so far, I will say that this is not a pleasant place to be. The feeling you get when you..."

He cut his words short as the chair next to him slid a few feet to his left, on its own. He turned to his left, startled, and sat up straight to look at the chair.

"I'm not sure if you could hear that, but the chair next to me just slid at least three feet to my left. Hello? Is anyone here with me? I am calling out, not to any demon or spirit, but to whoever may be in here. Someone has to be here."

Peter shined the light in all directions and saw no one. He stood to walk around.

"I said, is anyone here? If this is some kind of prank I will be very upset with Ritter and whoever may be involved."

This scared him. He walked into the kitchen and looked around, then down to the bathroom and turned on the light. He was determined to find out who was playing this joke on him. He didn't want to admit that this could be the work of something beyond our world.

"Alright, enough of this. I came here to experience this place and be objective about what I see and hear. If there is no other living person here with me, and I am truly alone, then I must be open-minded to what just occurred. I will take my seat again at the desk and make notes of what just happened, and of my feelings of what was going through my mind at the time. After all, this is in the name of research!"

Peter wrote down his experiences, and noted all that happened. He fired up his laptop and did some writing, while in the mood of the moment. This was what he had hoped for.

"It's not the most normal environment to write in, but it is highly appropriate and perfect for what I am writing."

As the pendulum clock on the far wall swung to 2:30 a.m. Peter closed the lid on his computer and left his note pad and pen on the desk. He gathered his recorder and flashlight just as his phone buzzed in his pocket. He pulled it out and saw that his wife has sent him a text message, asking if he is all right.

"Damn. I asked her not to disturb me so I can focus on this, but I know she is worried."

He types on his phone: 'I am ok…talk soon'.

"That should hold her until I get out of here in a few hours. My plan now is to go to the Ritter's bedroom and, as someone involved in the paranormal would do, go to a murder location in the house at the same time when the murder took place—the murder of Mary Ritter. That's this author's idea of investigating the possibility of spirits or demons here. I can feel, as I get closer to the top of the stairs, that the air is much colder. This is the second time I have experienced this."

He walked down the hall towards the bedroom, shining his light straight ahead and along the walls. Arriving at the doorway of the Ritter's bedroom, and just as he paused to speak, the door to the room slammed in his face. The shocked horror author jumped back.

"My God, the door to the bedroom just slammed shut right in front of me. Someone must be in there. Who's there? I'm tired of these pranks!"

Peter reached for the knob and tried to turn it. It won't turn. He leaned on the door and it began to rumble wildly on its hinges.

Startled, Keller stepped back. The rumbling stopped and the door slowly opened.

"What the hell? As I must describe what is happening, the door shook wildly as I tried to open it. I leaned on it and tried to turn the knob, to no avail. Then the shaking stopped and the door opened…on its own. Either this is a very good prank, or there is something very, very dreadful going on here." He paused. "No, no, it must a prank."

Keller charged into the room, shining the light in all directions.

"Whoever is here, show yourself."

"You better leave before it gets you too."

The voice came from behind Keller. He turned and saw the bloody body of Mary Ritter lying in bed, looking at him.

"Who? What the . . .?"

Mary threw her head back and laughed crazily, then slowly disappeared in front of Keller's eyes. The stunned and disbelieving author stared at the now empty bed.

"I...I...I am not sure what I just heard and saw. I don't know if it's my imagination or that I'm tired, but I just saw the ghost of Mary Ritter in her bed."

Keller paced the room and kept his flashlight shining on the bed.

"She spoke and in my disbelief, I am not exactly sure what she said. It was something to the effect of: *'They will get you too.'* I can't believe I'm even saying all this, but that is what I saw. It's freezing in here now."

Keller cautiously moves closer to the bed to have a better look.

"The bed looks undisturbed despite *just* seeing her lying there and..."

The closet door behind him opened and closed then slowly creaked open halfway.

"Leave this house. Leave this house now!"

A dark, demonic voice came from the closet. Keller stood quietly, not wanting to turn and see who, or what spoke those words. The voice recorder dropped from his hand as he built up the courage to turn.

Turning slowly, his eyes came into view of the closet door as it slammed shut. He was torn between running from the room, or keeping his bravado and opening the closet door. With his nerves rattled and feeling total distress, he decided to take a step towards the closet. The door rattled in front of him as he reached out. The white, porcelain knob felt cold to the touch, and in one swift motion, he turned it and opened the door.

"I have gathered myself and am going back downstairs. I lost my composure for a few moments and dropped my audio recorder. I have experienced something I cannot dispute. I have witnessed paranormal events in this house. They include visions, voices, and movement of solid objects that have no explanation. The time is now 3:30 a.m. and I will gather my thoughts at my desk and note all that has just happened."

"At approximately 3:00 a.m. the ghost or what appeared to be the ghost, of Mary Ritter spoke to me as she lay, bloody, in her bed. I played back the audio and she can clearly be heard telling me to *'leave before it gets me too'*. I must say even I cannot pass this off in some skeptical, scientific way. I saw and heard this very clearly, and now I have it recorded. She slowly disappeared into nothing after her warning to me. Soon after that, the closet door behind me opened and closed and a completely different voice, a very evil voice, told me to leave the house. I walked to the door, and will admit, that I was very scared. The door began to shake violently and when I grabbed the knob, the shaking stopped. I flung the door open and found no one or nothing inside. I have tried to pull the voice up on my recorder, which I had dropped just a moment before, but I have not been able to hear it. I will get this to the proper audio experts for analysis later today. I will take a moment now."

"I speak to you now from the kitchen; it is almost 4:00

a.m. I have scribbled on paper, the best I could, my account of my night thus far. Mostly, I have sat in a numbed state of mind and in thought. Nothing more has happened in the last hour or more. Before I came here I was not a skeptic to these types of things happening, but I wasn't a believer either. I wanted to come here, as I have stated before, to soak up, for my next novel, this so-called *evil* environment, based on the reputation of this place and because of the violent acts which have happened here. It does not matter if what I tell you is believable to you or not. What matters is that I know what I have experienced, and with that I know this place is indeed evil and persuasive. The evil that dwells here, in my opinion, is responsible for every violent murder that has occurred in this horrid place. Debra Blakely, sixty years ago, told all, the devil made her do it, I now believe her. My thoughts are this way, not only because of the things I have experienced physically, it's more than that. In the last hour I have been experiencing a mental weight or anguish. It comes from within, like a dark force driving at the mind and spirit. It is a pressure that is hard to describe, almost, if I dare say, like possession. I know I should leave this place now, as I was warned, but I am drawn to learn more, to see if I can bring out more visions of the past. I plan to leave here at 7:00 a.m., so I have roughly three hours to complete my stay and learn as much as I can."

"I now sit at the desk, but I am about to go upstairs and can again hear the loud thumping, or stepping. The steps are slow, but grow louder with each one. They are coming from beyond the kitchen, now moving closer. Whatever is making these sounds is clearly in this room."

Keller's voice was shaky and for the first time sounded frightened.

"I see no one with my light. I have chills, but I am sweating, I sense the dread and overpowering feeling of this evil entity. I know it is here with me, very close. The last step shook the wooden floor beneath me."

The walls begin shaking, the floor vibrated, and the desk began to rattle. A scared and shaking Peter Keller stumbled backwards and he tripped over a stool and lost the recorder and light. The house, from the windows to the walls, began to shake violently. Cries and screams rained down on him from all directions. The piercing cries of pain and suffering rang in his ears. Keller felt around for his only companion, his flashlight. He was almost in tears when he felt the light. He grabbed it and shined it all around the chaotic room.

The demons spoke to Peter. "Kill her. Kill her. Kill the bitch!" *He was shaking and sobbing, and covering his ears. Suddenly the house went calm. The noises and the horrible screaming stopped, and the house went deathly quiet. The only sound he could hear was his heart rapidly beating in his chest...until he heard the sound of a woman laughing from a distance. The laugh was not a normal laugh, it sounded crazed and deranged. He tried to gather himself from the shaking and shined the light towards the staircase. Peter's eyes grew wide as his light shined directly on a woman walking down the stairs. She carried an axe over her shoulder. She turned her head to him and he saw that her eyes were completely white. Peter was unable to move, frozen in place. The woman was standing over him in a split second and raised the axe above her to strike down on him. Despite his frightened state, he recognized her instantly!*

Debra Blakely!

"Kill her!" Debra commanded.

It was all too much for the author to take in. He passed out.

After waking up in a daze, a couple of hours later, Peter gathered his things and left the Ritter House behind. He arrived at his home in Chicago carrying a duffel bag over his shoulder. His wife Katherine was very much relieved, and after a very brief hello, Peter went to his bed to lie down. Katherine, feeling somewhat disappointed in not getting to hear about his night right away, decided to run some hot water for a bath.

A few minutes later, as Katherine lay in the tub with a warm rag over her eyes; Peter pushed the bathroom door open and walked in. He was carrying an axe. Katherine barely had time to remove the rag from her eyes before the first blow struck down on her chest. With the power and intensity of the blow, the axe easily cut into her chest and lodged deep inside. She didn't even have time to scream. The tub's soapy water began to turn a shade of crimson as the second blow from the axe landed with the same force and splattered blood all over the walls, mirrors, and floor of the once peaceful bathroom.

Peter left the axe wedged in Katherine's neck and calmly walked down the hall and into his room, picked up his phone, and dialed 911.

"911, what's your emergency?" the operator asked.

"I...I just killed my..." The 911 operator then heard him begin to weep.

"Sir? Are you there?" she asked. *She got no answer, only the sound of his weeping. She tried to get him to respond, and after a few seconds the operator listened as his cries turned into laughter, hysterical laughter. The laughter became louder and louder and more uncontrolled.*

The Chicago Police were dispatched, and when they arrived they got no answer at the door. They broke into the home of the world-famous horror author, Peter Keller. He was nowhere to be found. Katherine's body was found in the blood-filled tub, the axe still lodged deeply in her neck.

Upon searching the house, police heard voices coming from Peter's bedroom. After carefully entering, they found the audio recorder on his bed. The recording device was looping, playing over and over, a portion of what had been recorded at the Ritter House.

"Kill her. Kill her. Kill the bitch! Kill her. Kill her. Kill the...."

CHICAGO MIKE
by Della West

To be forewarned, is to be forearmed.

Should a pleasant but ordinary looking man approach you in the aisle of your local grocery store and strike up a conversation, be careful. Do not let your guard down for even an instant. For there is always the chance you are standing face to face with Chicago Mike.

It is not within my powers to save your life. All I am able to do is offer you the words of warning that are contained within my story. Do with them what you will.

One might say Chicago Mike is a house painter. A house painter with a twist that is. For you see, he only paints the inside of houses working in one medium….blood. To his nose the coppery aroma that accompanies the spilling of blood, is as intoxicating as the aroma rising from the city dumpsters is to the stray dogs and rodents that prowl the night.

The majority of people will by nature, wash their hands when they become coated with some foreign substance. But to Chicago Mike, blood is not something to wash off, it is indeed, something to be savored.

After coating his hands in the blood of his latest victim, he then sits and patiently waits for them to dry. Once dry, he applies another coat of the precious nectar. This ritual will be repeated precisely six times before he is able to stop. Now wearing his gloves of blood, he runs his fingers softly over the skin of his own face. It is a gesture he wishes the women in his life would do, but alas they never will, for they are all dead.

How does the human tongue describe what happens to a person when a very long nail, moves rapidly through the skin and bone of their skull? And then continues on into the brain, where it wipes out every memory and personality trait that has ever lived there?

Despite seeing himself as something of a ladies man, the truth is indeed quite different. But then his mind has always been inclined to mislead him. It is his mind after all, that tells him to approach various women in the grocery store. When he hesitates, his mind once again speaks, reminding him that he is the most attractive and sexy man who has ever lived. And despite having a mirror at home, he falls for it every time.

Now filled to the brim with self-confidence, he marches right up to her. A woman who is simply trying to get one more errand done, so she can go home and possibly have a single moment to herself. A minute of peace and quiet, before her family members hit the door like a herd of buffalo.

While it can be any woman at any Walmart, one thing never changes, the revulsion the women all feel as they see this homely and dumpy man standing next to her, wearing a lopsided and leering smile upon his overly wet lips.

"There is no need to say it, I already know you want me."

Here is where the reactions of the women would differ. Some of them would simply clutch more tightly to their handbags, and make their way quickly down the aisle. It was the other reaction that always led to the trouble.

The laughter. Some of them would actually laugh at him. To his twisted way of thinking, this reaction made no sense. Hadn't his mind just assured him he was the most desirable man to ever live?

The desire in her eyes was just as clear as a glass of water. Body language says a lot and her body said "*take me, I'm yours.*" How dare she set him up in such a cruel way! If the word of a woman meant no more than that, what earthly good was she?

This person who a few moments ago was doing her grocery shopping, has somehow become enmeshed in a game that no one else knows the rules to. This odd man who stands before her with the strangest of looks upon his face, seems to be the holder of the rule book. She has no idea why he looks so angry, nor of the incredible danger she is in.

And so it goes. Eventually he will drift away, but he will not go far. Just an aisle or two, so that she will feel as if the threat has passed. She has no way of knowing the threat has only just begun.

The encounter with the strange angry man has receded to the back of her mind. Busily loading the bags of groceries into the trunk, the woman never thinks to look over her shoulder. But for him, it is a much different situation. For her cruel lie, is now the only thought his fractured mind is able to grasp ahold of. As he follows behind her in his rattle-trap car, she is blissfully unaware of the drastically awful change that is about to take place in her world.

The few minutes she was so looking forward to having alone, would prove to be more than enough time for Chicago Mike to accomplish his work. He would make her see the error of her ways. All he wanted to do, was to convince her that he was the sexiest, most desirable man she had ever seen. Why had she insisted on making a simple situation so hard?

Pulling into the garage, her mind was now way beyond anything that had happened at the grocery store. After all, weird people are not exactly in short supply, and one cannot get upset every time one of them crosses your path.

In just a moment or two, it would all come flooding back, striking her brain like a nail gun pointed into her ear and fired, as a matter of fact that is exactly the fate awaiting her. He had to make her see, how wrong and unkind it was to reject a fellow human being.

For years to come, family and friends would speculate about just what kind of person would perform such a demented act upon someone who they all loved so much. What kind of mind would be capable of sending, a long nail shooting through the brain of such a well-liked woman?

The answers they all craved would remain hidden from sight. Oh, there would be a lot of speculation and some just plain guesses, but the truth would remain a secret known only by their departed loved one and Chicago Mike.

What the crime scene investigators found nearly as unnerving as the bizarre murder itself, was how the killer had taken the time to paint the walls inside the bedroom red. No one who stood at the crime scene that day, needed a Luminal test to tell them that his paint brush had been dipped in blood.

The smell of copper in the air was overwhelming. Nearly bringing tears to the eyes of all who had the misfortune of spending several hours in this room. If one was able to look past the carnage, they would see that earlier in the day this had been a lovely bedroom. A room that had been decorated in very good taste, but was now in a state of horror.

The woman lies crumpled in a heap upon the plush

carpeting, covered in so much blood it seemed one body could not have held it all. With her neck elongated just as far as possible, she gave the appearance of one who tried to get as far away from the projectile as possible, without actually moving her body.

One astute crime scene investigator pointed out, if you followed the path of her now dead and staring eyes, they led straight to a Bible that had been knocked off of the nightstand and landed face up on the floor. One of the toughest and most grizzled homicide detectives the police force had, spoke in a voice so soft that it almost went unheard. "I hope it was a comfort to her."

Had his victim still been alive, she could have offered the women of America some very valuable advice. Do not laugh at Chicago Mike.

It was the women who he managed to get inside of his house he enjoyed the most. Even if they did not realize it quite yet, he knew they all loved him. They would come around to his way of thinking, after a little of his special persuading. After all, when not constrained by the morays of society, he had the power to be quite convincing.

While he did not possess the conventional charm and smoothness of a leading man in a Hollywood film, what he did have were his own tools of persuasion. He was aware his methods would be considered by most people to be harsh and possibly even cruel, but it had never been his way to adjust his style to the approval of other people. He was after all, Chicago Mike.

As he went about his daily routine, his mind raced with a myriad of thoughts. But the one played out the most frequently was, *if he was such a loser with the ladies, how come they never left him?* All over the world, women were leaving their husbands and boyfriends. Sometimes for other men and sometimes because they found being alone was better than what they had been putting up with for years. "Yet his ladies stayed, say what you will, he hadn't lost one yet."

He was pretty sure the reason they never left was because he treated them like precious works of art. Something you held in your possession so beautiful, it rendered you speechless as well as breathless on a daily basis.

That is why he had developed his special method of preserving the ones he loved. As he would work on them, he would explain that they were getting a spa treatment. The fact that the arms, legs and head he was massaging, were no longer attached to a torso, seemed of little importance to his mind.

Anyone could see his work was exquisite. The care he gave to each and every detail required the greatest of focus. Chicago Mike would place his precious jewel with care upon the work station. Just what was this treasure he handled with such incredible care? A human head. Always being gentle and polite, he would begin the long and painstaking process of removing the skin from the muscle and bones.

This was a much nicer environment to work in than those of his offsite jobs. For even with his considerable skills, the damage done by the nail gun would not allow him to create perfection. And after all, a master craftsman must always work his hardest to maintain a high standard of quality once you start to slack off, your sales will follow the same downward path.

Through a great deal of trial and error, he developed a process. It required the utmost care, as the market had become accustomed to his work being of the very finest quality. It would only take putting out shoddy work once or twice, before he would be out of business entirely. That would never do, for he was a true artist. A master craftsman in his chosen field.

Chicago Mike had lost count of the compliments he had received, but never the warm way the praise had made him feel inside. It had at first been difficult to let any of his women go. But he did have bills to pay, and he had assured them that his love would remain strong, even though they would live at someone else's house.

But there were always those who would never be sold, no matter how much profit he stood to make. These ones would remain with him forever. They were his soul mates.

As the process continued at its very slow and deliberate pace, he would talk to the head he held gently in his hands. "You do know how much I love you, don't you?" he would ask in a whiney tone of voice which fairly begged the lifeless head to answer. As if beseeching her to give him the reassurance of love and affection his troubled mind had always so desperately craved.

"Of course there have been others before you, and surely there will be more to come." He would explain while looking deeply into the dead eyes staring back at him. He would now begin to worry his sweetheart could be having second thoughts about being in love with him.

Speaking softly while he gently stroked the hair laid out across a table to his left, he quickly attempts to provide his true love an explanation that will make everything right once again. "What do you expect me to do? I am after all Chicago Mike, the sexiest man to ever have lived. Is it my fault if the ladies find me irresistible? Worry not my darling, for no matter how many others there may be, you are the one that I love."

Pausing for a moment to listen, he concludes this hastily put together explanation must have done the trick, for he hears no sound or argument. He can now get on with transforming his beloved into something truly special.

The city of Chicago has a long and interesting history, stretching back for well over one hundred years before it became incorporated in the year 1833. Having been discovered in 1673, it would be the scene of many interesting historical events, both happy and sad.

Many are the changes and upheavals have crossed the paths of those who have called this Illinois city home: from the Fort Dearborn Massacre and the Great Chicago Fire, to the White Sox sweeping of the World Series in 2005.

It is a place of both pride and shame; many accomplishments have taken place here, both good and bad. Contributions that would benefit society as a whole, as well as a crime rate which has forced the citizens to adapt to living with an uncomfortable level of fear.

But long before the spike in violent street crime, there was a sense of fear among the people. For it would seem as if someone was preying upon the women of Chicago. These crimes resulted in a feeling no one was truly safe anywhere they went, or even at home for that matter.

Workmen on construction sites would hide their nail guns within their pickup trucks, until they got to work. More than one construction worker had been rattled by the look of pure panic on the face of a woman in the next vehicle, who just happened to glance at the seat of his truck. Only to catch sight of a nail gun.

Of the many stores which fill the Water Tower Place Mall, there is one that fascinates the shoppers most of all. No one would disagree, the man who owns the shop is something of an oddball. But in some strange way his peculiar manner seems to add to the ambiance of the place. Besides, he is not scary in any way, just a bit weird.

The neon sign above the door reads, *Hiding in Plain Sight Costumes*. Never does a person enter into this store and leave without having made mention of just how life-like the masks are. Shoppers often feel compelled to reach out and touch the masks, in a desire to see if they are as soft as they look. Without fail they all make exactly the same wonder-filled comment, "It feels just like real skin!"

Face masks, or masks made of faces, are not the only unique items sold at Hiding in Plain Sight. No indeed, there are also the gloves. You should hear the comments people make when picking them up and trying them on. "It feels as if you are not even wearing gloves." "It is as if you are slipping your hands into a pair of hands, so natural is the fit."

These comments always brought a quiet chuckle from Chicago Mike. For just because he was diabolical and a bit nuts, did not mean that he could not appreciate irony. No one ever seemed to take note of the pleased expression spread across the shop owner's face, but then so few people ever notice Chicago Mike at all.

The shopping public will, it seems, pay a great deal of money for a costume if the mask is incredibly life-like. And while it does break his heart to see one of his true loves go to another home, a dollar is after all, a dollar.

But he always takes the utmost of care when wrapping the mask in tissue paper before putting it in the bag and handing it over to the customer. He makes sure to let his fingers run gently across the cheek one final time, as he whispers a heartfelt farewell.

As satisfied customers make their way out through the door, heading for the food court, something catches the eye of Chicago Mike. A blank spot on the wall. Staring at the empty space, he hears the voice within his mind begin to speak, "time to go out and collect a new love." And so the process begins all over again. *Perhaps this time she will not laugh. If only they would not laugh.*

Since the beginning of mankind, there have always

existed the unfortunate ones. People who for whatever reason, never seemed quite able to find their place in this world. Everyone is born with a niche carved out just for them, why some people seem unable to ever locate theirs, is a mystery that has confounded society from the beginning of time.

These sad souls live on the outskirts of life and seem to exist in a fog. This fog has a variety of origins. For some it comes from drugs or alcohol. For others the source of the fog is mental illness, holding them prisoner in a prison as secure as the Tamms Correctional Center.

The street corners of every city are littered with what remains of these lost people. Easy picking for anyone with a few dollars in their pocket, and a car in which they can sit for a short time. Hopefully long enough for the chill to leave their bones and the feeling to return to their fingers and toes. That wind will surely cut like a knife as they stand out in it and wait for a lustful predator to drive up and offer to buy a piece of their soul.

They are the low hanging fruit and the easiest pickings of all, for someone like Chicago Mike. These women are much less inclined to laugh at him, or to slowly begin edging away while trying to hide their revulsion. Their lives are filled with revolting people. Mean, selfish people they must spend time very, very close to.

He always made sure to stop and pick up something for the woman to eat, before making his way to the strip of boulevard that wound its way through the red light district. Something deep fried and aromatic, like french fries, always worked like magic. Add to that the offer of a higher payday for the quickest of work, along with a warm house they would be more than welcome to spend the night in, and one could expect a near stampede to the open car door.

Once back at the house, Chicago Mike will offer his

guest a hot bath and a cold drink. Both of which will be readily accepted by this woman who must surely feel as if she has somehow been transported to Oz.

While luxuriating in the tub full of bubbles and sipping the beverage, she will hardly notice she is becoming sleepy. After all, when one spends every minute of every day fighting a battle against life, weariness is a constant companion.

Within a few minutes she will be out cold, and he will take the glass from her hand a split second before her head slips below the water level. The sedative and the bathwater will do the job for him, leaving behind a canvas without mar.

Once the small bubbles have ceased to rise from the submerged nostrils, Chicago Mike will reach into the water and give a firm pull on the chain. The chain will in turn pull on the beige colored rubber plug, and the water will begin its descent into the drain.

Once all of the water is gone, he will sit on the bathroom counter and begin a dialog with his latest true love. "I always knew I would find you some day. Such a naughty girl to be out on those dirty streets, doing those dirty things. How fortunate it is, that I came along just in time to save you. Didn't your mother ever warn you about the dangers of living and working on the streets? Yes, you are indeed blessed I came along and chose you for my true love."

Over the course of several days, he will work diligently to remove the wear and tear that over the years of hard living, has marked her face with lines and sadness. He will in time transform her into a work of art. A thing of beauty he can love and treasure for all time.

He will give her a new name as well, wiping away all traces of her past. No longer will she be known as Claudia, the streetwalking drug addict. From this day forward she will be known as Victoria, fine lady and love of his life.

It is a sadly strange truth Claudia's quality of life dramatically improved, the moment she died. For finally, somebody truly loved her. Had she not faded away at the bottom of a bathtub, she would have most assuredly been pleased with the name Victoria, as well as someone sincerely loving her. Even if it was a twisted sort of devotion.

Chicago Mike decided this one would never be sold. She would be given a place of honor in his home and they would spend the rest of their days together. It would be nice to have someone to talk to in the morning while he drank his morning coffee. Being alone all of the time can really take a toll on a man's state of mind.

The process used to turn these unfortunate women into masquerade masks, is really quite complicated and ingenious. Involving many steps and a great deal of delicate handiwork. It took a lot of practice and adjusting formulas and methods, but Chicago Mike finally got it perfected.

Chicago Mike is gone. No one knows where he has gone or why he left. He simply closed his shop, packed up his treasures and disappeared among the more than 300 million people who call America home.

In closing, I offer you this simple but heartfelt advice. Should you ever be approached by a non-descript man who speaks with a Midwestern accent, while doing your grocery shopping, proceed with extreme caution. And please, whatever you do, don't laugh.

THE GHOSTS OF MORSE
by Julianne Snow

T he hallway bustled with hundreds of teenagers all changing classes at once. The tide moved in both directions as backpacks and shoulders jostled for position.

"Hey! Dan!"

Daniel Butler turned toward the voice, stopping his progress through the door to his history class. Seeing his best friend, he smiled, "Hey Nate! What's up?"

"Not much, just on my way to biology." Nate pulled a face, showing his disdain for the subject in question, "It's dissection day and I really don't want to go."

"But dissecting the frog was the highlight of that class! Made all the boring stuff worth it in the end."

"Dude, you know I have no problems with the rest of the class, I just don't want to cut open some stupid frog."

"You're still scared of them aren't you?" Daniel looked at his friend but couldn't help the laughter from welling up inside him. It spilled from him before he could stop it and the resultant blush that flushed Nate's pale face was answer enough.

"C'mon, you would've been scared too if you got trapped inside that cave! Freaking frogs everywhere, jumping all over me! In The Dark!" He shivered at the memory of the night that had happened almost seven years ago now. "Besides, you're afraid of worms so shut it!"

Daniel had to give that one to him as he detested worms with a passion. "Yeah, yeah…" was his attempt to brush it off.

"Anyway, you still want to have that party this weekend? Gary can totally get us a few brews from work."

"Absolutely! But we're going to need to find a new place to hold it. My mom said we can't drink in the backyard anymore since the new neighbours complained."

"Complained?"

"Yeah, said we were too loud and that next time they'd call the police. Mom just doesn't want any trouble, so we need to find a new place."

Nate shifted his backpack higher on his shoulder while he thought, "Let me think about it and maybe we can figure something out after class?"

"Sure thing dude. Now go cut that frog open and show him who's boss!"

Nate shot him a grimace and turned to continue down the hall, his body seeming to lag in the quick flow of student traffic. The second bell rung signalling the final minute before class would begin. Taking his seat, a great idea hit Daniel. He knew where they could party this coming weekend—a place with a past, but free of any form of authority.

In his brain it was decided. The field next to the old Morse Train Station was the perfect backdrop for a little teenage fun.

◊ ◊ ◊ ◊

"So what did your brother score us?" Daniel eagerly scanned the back of Nate's father's car looking at the cases which sat there. Gary, his older brother, worked for the Bent River Brewing Company in nearby Rock Island, and from time to time he could be bribed into bringing home a few free samples. Most of the kids didn't care the beer had been obtained via the five finger discount; they only cared about the buzz it'd give them and the resulting hours where they could forget about their small town existence.

"We've got a few cases of Paddle Wheel and Dry Hopped for us," Nate relayed while showing off the haul his brother had snuck out of the brewery. "And for the ladies, there's some Raspberry Wheat."

"Fucking-A!"

"Yeah, Gary really came through for us this time. Now we just need to get to Morse and get this party started!" Nate and Daniel high-fived in excitement. While they preferred to party close to home, they couldn't run the risk the police would break up their get together for underage drinking. While the teenagers liked to have fun, they were still responsible, opting for overnight bonfires instead of the other alternative. They all remembered the accident from 2011—the one that took the lives of Rodney Turnbull, Shelley Wright, and Hector Franx. Plus it was the only way they could continue the arrangement with Gary; in return for beer, they'd had to promise they wouldn't put their lives in danger.

Closing the hatchback of the car after placing their sleeping bags and cooler full of sandwiches and snacks for the night inside, the two hopped into the front to begin the journey that would only take them a few miles out of Bradford, Illinois.

◊ ◊ ◊ ◊

With the bonfire burning, the tents set up around the field, and the first beers partway down the throats of the less parched group, the laughter and conversation flowed easily. Groups came together, then split in an ever-changing rotation of friends.

"Hey, anyone want to hear a ghost story?" The question came from Susan Boyd, one of the more vocal students at the Bureau Valley High School. Her many extra-curricular activities included starring in each production of the Drama Club.

As the young adults began to gather round, Susan took her place with beer in hand. She took a deep breath and began.

"So, many of you know that Morse used to be a bustling town, right?"

The crowd gathered around her all nodded, the history of the town nothing new to them.

"Well, the railroad used to come through the middle of town, stopping many times throughout the day to drop off passengers and freight. Heck, the rail line is still active, though there are fewer trains than what there used to be."

"Get to the story Susan!"

"Patience, patience!" She said it with a smile though everyone knew Susan was annoyed by the interruption. "Here's the scary part, the trains aren't scheduled to come through the area at night. Part of the 'community quietening' initiative that's been popular lately."

"How is that scary?" Daniel couldn't help but ask the question through a pull of his beer.

"Good question!" she paused to smile at him. "Well, locals have reported hearing the train's whistle at night and seeing lights. When the police check things out there's no evidence of a train coming through or of one even being on the tracks at that time."

A collective noise of awe spread through the group, some of the kids jostling each other in the hopes of eliciting a scream or two of terror. But there was more laughter that night than screams as the fun and games started in earnest. With many of the teenagers occupied in conversation or throwing around Frisbees, there didn't seem to be a care in the world among them.

In the distance the eerily but beautiful ghost of the whistle sounded, coming closer by the second.

All eyes turned in the direction of the sound, a hush falling over the group. Teenagers moved imperceptibly closer together, the chill of the sound causing them to seek the warmth of others.

As one they scanned the horizon across the field, staring in the direction of the tracks, waiting but not wanting to see the lights of the train. The first flicker of the lights set them into a panic, the group scattering as if the train would pass right through the field they were using.

"Holy fucking shit!" It was Nate who said the words they were all thinking. Even as they scattered, they watched for the full lights of the train, not wanting to know, but needing to see nonetheless.

But the lights didn't materialize into anything, they just simply flickered then died behind the break of the trees. The group stopped to stare, expecting the lights to trick them by bursting forth as the train barrelled down on them.

There was nothing.

"Okay, that was insane! Who wants to go with me to take a look?" Susan was standing in the middle of the crowd when she made her bold challenge. "We can just walk over to the tracks by the road and then walk up them until we get to the trees."

No one answered her, all of them still a little too freaked to be the second brave one of the group.

"Are you kidding me? None of you have the balls to go?" The firelight reflected off her face, showcasing the look of incredulity on it. "What about you Nate? You game?"

Nate shuffled his feet in the grass, not wanting to look like a chicken in front of everyone, but not wanting to venture out in the darkness either. He looked at Daniel before shrugging his shoulders, "Sure I guess."

"Awesome! Anyone else interested in coming?" A few other teens opted for the midnight sleuthing session and the cadre strode off across the field armed with flashlights. The rest of the group warily got back to the party, everyone's nerves just a little more on edge.

◊ ◊ ◊ ◊

On the tracks, Nate had to ask, "What do you hope to find Susan? Evidence there really is a ghost train?"

"I don't know, but you have to admit that was totally freaky!"

"Yeah, definitely freaky…" Howard Shaw was the one who spoke. As one of the running backs on the football team, he figured it was best the group have a little muscle while away from the party. There was no telling what was out there in the dark waiting for them.

They trudged up the tracks, careful not to trip or wedge their feet into the tight spaces between the iron rails, each of them lost in their own thoughts. Speech was attempted, but soon fell off into silence as the stupidity of what they were doing became more apparent.

Up ahead there was a faint flicker of blinding white light.

◊ ◊ ◊ ◊

The hauntingly beautiful sound of the train whistle broke the noise of the party once again. It's strident keening louder and longer this time. It sounded like a warning and each of the faces around the fire felt the difference in its tone.

They stared again as the lights of the locomotive broke through the copse of trees and barrelled down the tracks, disappearing into the inky blackness beyond the edge of the ghost town. The echo of a scream reverberated against the trees all around the field, raising gooseflesh and ancillary hairs all over their bodies.

The group descended into "What the fuck?", "I thought there wasn't supposed to be trains running at night?", and "Did you just see what I saw?" before going quiet again, each one of them lost for a moment in their own thoughts. They tried desperately to come to terms with what they'd just seen, but no answers were forthcoming. It was the most terrifyingly strange thing any of them had ever witnessed.

"Has anyone heard from Nate or the others since they left?" Daniel asked as the light from his screen illuminated the look of worry on his face.

The field lit up as the teens all checked their phones, now desperate to have heard from their friends.

No one had received anything.

"Okay, we need to go and look for them."

"Can't we just text them and wait to see if they answer? There's no point in us going out there if they're on their way back."

Daniel couldn't fault the logic of the suggestion and called Nate's phone. In the distance the chords of *Thunderstuck* played as he waited for his friend to connect.

The song continued to play, uninterrupted.

Daniel disconnected before Nate's voicemail engaged and tried again, hearing the same chords bounce out of the darkness at him. Soon they were joined by the ringtones of the others who had gone to investigate. The cacophony retreated into silence as the voicemail for each picked up.

"Okay, so it's decided. We're going to go look."

"They're probably out there just waiting to scare the pants off of us."

"It doesn't matter if they are, we still need to go and look."

Daniel set off from the group in the direction of the tracks not really caring who followed him. He just wanted to find his friend and make sure he was safe. A part of him believed the train was real, unable to accept that such a thing could be ghosting along the tracks. And if it were a real train, it was possible his friends had been hurt. Besides, he couldn't have been the only one to have heard the scream that rushed out of the darkness at them as the train passed by.

Reaching the tracks, Daniel scanned the ground with the light from his cellphone. None of them had any flashlights, having realized the first group had taken them all with them. Was it suspect? Of course. But Daniel had a sinking feeling something just wasn't right.

He began to walk down the tracks, scanning his light left and right as he looked for clues. The others followed along behind him, looking for anything he might have missed, but also keeping an eye out for the lights of the next train.

They moved forward, eerily aware they couldn't hear the party any longer. The sounds of their heightened breathing loud in their ears.

"I found something," Daniel said from a few feet in front of the rest. They rushed to catch up with him to see the cracked screen of a cellphone laying in the gravel and weeds between the rails. Picking it up to look at it, he ran his finger over its damaged face. "It's not covered in dirt and it still works so it's not been here for long."

"That's Howard's phone."

"Okay, so chances are they're not too far in front of us."

"Why wouldn't Howard stop to pick up his phone? With a crack like that it's pretty likely he heard it fall to the ground. Heck, he probably even felt it drop."

Daniel considered the question for a moment as he scanned the darkness before them. They could see a few feet of tracks before they disappeared into the night. "Let's try calling their phones again."

The ringtones polluted the air again as the area around them lit up with the screens of the ringing cellphones. Stepping back, the small group scanned the tracks and adjacent grass for the technology, careful not to step on anything that looked important.

"What does this me—"

The question was interrupted by another whistle, this one louder and closer. The group looked up just as the light broke through the trees ahead of them. The sound was intense, the vibrations on the ground shaking their resolve. But they all stood there, frozen as the light bore down on them.

◊ ◊ ◊ ◊

The train whistle would sound twice more that night, each time more teenagers would go in search of their friends.

A few of them were smart, refusing to go off because none of the others came back. Calling the police at some point during the night, the remaining teens told the story of the train whistle and their friends who'd gone in search of it. The officers could find no trace of the students except for discarded cellphones in the fields.

Hundreds of them scattered, all of them damaged.

Locals still hear the train's whistle at night. But they also hear the ghosts of Morse ringing on the winds.

DROWNING IN THE HAZEL
by Eli Constant

L etting go of everything, that's what diving felt like, balancing below the water, breathing in and out slowly and watching the small stream of bubbles escape and head toward the surface. Sometimes, Lillian Miles wanted to stay below forever, never follow those bubbles upward, never break the water's surface again and just…sleep. That would be easier than moving forward from the life-altering changes of the past months.

◊ ◊ ◊ ◊

She was at the very deepest point of the chlorine-rich pool, looking up at the way the light outside the water played through the waves, moving and refracting. Lillian's body felt heavy, yet buoyant. The soft weights in her buoyancy vest kept her low, her back brushing the concrete floor, but her arms and legs and head and heart floated listlessly, freely, up and down with the small wakes in the water made by other swimmers.

Diving consumed her thoughts nowadays, ever since the impromptu trip to Cabo San Lucas she'd taken with her mother, sister and closest friend as a 'my fiancé just dumped me' getaway. All of Lillian's companions had seen the three-day diving course as the perfect tourist option and it had started out that way for Lillian too, but once she'd sunken below the rocking ocean waves, everything had come into perspective. Life had come into perspective. Mel had come into perspective.

Melvin McCray. Lillian's entire family had been astonished when he'd proposed after only eight months. She'd never had a real 'prospect,' as her mother Tess called marriageable men with money; she'd never even dated a man longer than a few months. Lillian's mother cited fundamental personality issues. Lillian's sister, Gail, just said she needed to spruce herself up a bit, act like she gave a damn about her appearance, apply a touch of lipstick, dress in the best colors for her skin tone. Of course Gail would say that, being a makeup artist at the mall—all she ever thought about was physical aesthetics, no need to search below the surface when the outward appearance can be made pretty.

That's why Lillian felt so free below the water. She loved how the wetness always washed away every trace of the most recent Gail-intervention-makeover. Water only let the most superficial, air-filled things rule its surface. Everything else of substance sank beneath, to rest on the bottom, to be found by people willing to explore. Lillian looked at her pressure gauge; its hose, leading toward the first stage of her tank, was secured to her buoyancy vest by a rubber tie. She had a half-hour of air left—just enough time for her to close her eyes and forget.

◊ ◊ ◊ ◊

She had really thought Mel loved her. They'd met at a charity auction; his gallery in Chicago had donated a few pieces to the event. Lillian had been there representing the law firm. They'd bonded instantly, laughing and bantering like longtime friends. The two hour distance between Chicago and Champaign had never proven an obstacle and he was always so kind, so generous, quickly filling her once empty jewelry armoire with glittering prizes, material professions of love.

Then he'd come to her office three months ago to fetch her for a late lunch and he'd met Pamela-the-perfect, all legs, blonde locks and an infectious personality. Lillian had known, from the instant Mel had laid eyes on Pamela, from the moment Pamela had thrown her head back and laughed that tinkling-of-bells laugh, she'd known. It was only a matter of time. Sometimes, Lillian wished Pamela had attended the charity auction, met Mel first and saved Lillian loads of heartache.

At least Mel had the decency to break off the engagement before pursuing Pamela. He was at least that honorable. Not honorable enough to avoid Lillian's office though. Three or four times a week, Mel would drop by or send flowers or call wanting to talk to Pamela. He'd moved closer to Champaign to be closer to Pamela. To make matters worse, Lillian was Pamela's assistant. She got to buzz her boss and tell her Mel had arrived for lunch or answer the ringing phone, ask who was calling and then endure the *'Hello, Lillian. Hope you are well. Is Pamela in?"* The sound of her ex-fiancé's voice was nauseating now.

She'd found out Mel and Pamela were together a week after he'd asked for the engagement ring back. He hadn't told her. Instead, he'd sent a large bouquet of flowers to the office—purple-dipped white roses. Purple was Lillian's favorite color. She'd thought the flowers were for her, that Mel wanted to reconcile. She'd kept them on her desk for hours.

Then Pamela had walked up and plucked out a small ivory note; it had been buried deep in the bouquet and

Lillian hadn't seen it. After quickly reading the message, Pamela had picked up the flowers without a word and taken them to her office. She'd left the note written in Mel's penmanship sitting on the pale brown desk top. Subconsciously or consciously, Pamela had wanted Lillian to know that there wasn't any hope of getting Mel back. The contents of the note made that perfectly clear.

"I didn't know what love was before you, Pam. You are my life."

Lillian was rinsing the chlorine off her dive equipment in the women's locker room now, monopolizing the largest shower stall. She'd already rinsed her body and washed her hair; her small frame was wrapped in a thin white towel, her feet donning old pink sandals. After rinsing, she shoved everything except her yellow, aluminum tank into a large, tightly woven mesh duffel bag. The material didn't look strong, but it was woven out of the same stuff used in bullet-proof vests.

A second bag sat on a wood bench just outside the shower stall, where it would stay nice and dry. Towel-clad Lillian pushed back the shower curtain and went to the bench. Unzipping the bag and rummaging for a moment, she extracted undergarments, a pale pink blouse and black slacks. She dressed quickly and then ran her fingers through her still-wet hair. She didn't have time to dry the long black locks, so she twisted it up into a messy bun and secured it with a hair tie. Lastly, she took out the delicate sterling earrings she'd purchased in Cabo and put them on. She rocked her head gently, letting the little silver mermaids play against her chin line. They always made her smile.

Leaving on her pink sandals, she had comfortable kitten heels in the car; Lillian lugged her belongings out of the locker room and toward the aquatic center's exit. Fred waved to her on her way out; she smiled back, not willing to drop her heavy load for nicety's sake. He was a nice man, all white hair and mild manners and always seemed to be sitting in the same place, checking membership IDs and reading the newspaper—like a permanent fixture of the center. The only thing that ever really changed was the date on that newspaper; today was Thursday and Lillian wondered what the old man found within the crisp folds of the black-ink printed paper.

Putting all her gear in the back of her minivan—she'd traded in her two-door for the van after falling in love with scuba divining—she pulled down the rear hatch and jumped into the driver's seat. She'd have to soak the gear again at home, push it down into a bathtub full of lukewarm water then leave it several hours; otherwise, it would begin to smell damp and moldy from not drying properly after the pool.

The Urbana Indoor Aquatics Center was a large facility about three miles outside Champaign. The price wasn't bad and Lillian could swim, or practice her dive skills, from 6 AM to 8 AM before heading downtown to work. Champaign, Illinois was a beautiful little metropolis. About eighty thousand people moving in and out of each other's lives, the streets vibrating and expanding, but managing to retain some of the beauty of the past that some cities lose with the process of growth and modernization.

Lillian's favorite spot was the Art Theater on West Church Street. It was such a beautiful movie theater, all maroon brick and glazed, ivory arches, scalloped tile cornices and strong columns. It was easy to see that a lot of planning and love went into the design. You could walk into the building and instantly smell a hundred years of history, a century of popcorn and people sitting too close to one another. Over the years, the simplistic art deco theme survived—the concrete floor with deep red carpet, gray and white walls featuring large circles and painted rectangles—everything about the interior echoed a bygone era, full of playful abstraction.

The movies were the best part of the theater. No million dollar blockbuster movies, but true, artistic productions—independent films showcasing life and love and war in the very rawest and realest forms. Lillian always drove past the theater to get to work. Technically, it wasn't on the way to her job, but lately she needed that building; it was a reminder that even old, quirky things come to life with new love and possibility.

Passing by the Art Theater today, Lillian blew the old girl a kiss and then took the left turn to correct her course toward Stein, Green & Lord Law Firm. All she had to do was get through today at work, smile and try not to lose her mind. She'd taken Friday off and first thing in the morning, she'd be on her way to Mermaid Springs, her first diving adventure since Cabo San Lucas. Deborah, Lillian's best gal pal, was supposed to come along, but had canceled on Tuesday, saying Barry didn't want her to go and, frankly, she didn't trust him with their three kids anyway.

Lillian had expected as much. Deborah was at a different stage in her life—middle-aged, like her, but a decade married with kids and a cookie-cutter house in the suburbs. She was always canceling movie dates and shopping trips. That's just what happens when one friend gets married and settles down while the other remains single and 'looking.' It had been miraculous that Deb hadn't backed out on the Cabo trip.

The parking spot Lillian usually occupied was taken this morning, so she pulled around the block and parked the car in the business lot across from *Guido's*, her favorite spot for burgers and beer. The walk back to the office was short; the morning air was a little crisp for mid-August, but the day would warm up. She still wore her sandals, but had her heels in her oversized purse for office wear. The Weather Channel had said a high of 74° with the weekend being clear and sunny, perfect for the trip. Of course, Deborah canceling had put a little kink in the works. She was supposed to be Lillian's dive buddy.

Midwest Scuba had set up the dive trip to Mermaid Springs. Bernie, the dive master, hadn't accepted the 3-day certification course Lillian and Deb had taken in Cabo. He'd made them sit through an hour long slide-show on dive safety after he'd found out that they thought they were already trained and ready to hit the water. The presentation had been chocked-full of images of injured divers who didn't go down with a buddy or decompressed incorrectly, or ran out of air because they didn't know how to read the gauge. It was a wakeup call and both women had immediately signed up for Midwest's PADI certification course. It took about three weeks to complete and Lillian had supplemented the learning with practice at the aquatic center.

Bernie had been pretty gracious about Deborah backing out of the trip; he should be, considering the trip deposit was nonrefundable. On the downside, Lillian was now stuck with the older man as her dive buddy. Everyone else going on the trip was already paired up. Bernie was an okay guy, not terrible looking, but a bit overzealous for Lillian's taste. She knew he'd want to do safety checks three and four times before hitting the water and then double check each other's gear before descending.

She could get over that though; learn to love Bernie and all his paranoid precautions, if it meant sinking below the water and feeling free. Still…she wished he'd chosen to pair her with one of his staff. She had the feeling that Bernie wanted to dive with her; she grimaced, hoping the weekend wasn't going to turn into an endless onslaught of unwanted advances from the older man.

The door to the firm's office was propped open, letting in the cool morning breeze. Marianne, Mr. Green's law clerk, already sat at her desk, filing her nails. Lillian waved at her then made a beeline for her oak desk. She quickly glanced at Pamela's door. It was still closed, the office dark. The shiny, silver plaque on the wall next to Pamela's office said 'Pamela Lord, Attorney.' The only thing Lillian found comical about the whole Mel-Pamela situation was that Pamela specialized in divorce and common-law marriage cases. It just seemed fitting.

Sliding off her sandals, Lillian took her black kitten heels out of her bag and slipped them onto her feet, using the desk for support. The heels were only an inch high; she'd never felt comfortable walking in anything taller. She wished she did though; high heeled shoes were so feminine. The right pair of sling backs or peep toes could mean the difference between grabbing and repelling attention. At least, that's what Gail always said. As much as Lillian hated her sister's constant advice on looking more womanly, she couldn't help feeling like maybe her sister was right, maybe she didn't make enough of an effort to look the part of the dateable lady.

After grabbing a cup of Earl Grey with sugar and cream, Lillian sat down at her desk. Her black rolling chair squeaked in protest as she moved closer to the tabletop and began her morning ritual of checking messages, typing up memos and drafting case documents. As per usual, Pamela had left a mile high stack of folders she'd pulled for reference. That would take about an hour to re-file; sometimes, Lillian thought Pamela did it on purpose, because some of the files were on old cases that had long been settled and had no similarities to current cases. Maybe it was her boss's way of making little digs at her, mocking her ability to keep a boyfriend's interest. *Shut up, Lil, you're being stupid. Mel's long gone.* Lillian reprimanded herself.

She wouldn't let herself wallow anymore. Life goes on; she had new interests, new prospects and no interest in men at all. *Sure, keep telling yourself that.* Lillian rolled her eyes and huffed, unhappy at her inability to lie to even herself.

The best part about the upcoming weekend trip was the timing—Lillian's mom had called on Wednesday, finally restarting her old tradition of setting Lillian up weekend after weekend on blind date after blind date. It had given Lillian great satisfaction to tell her mother that she already had a date, a date with a full tank of air and cool hazel water. Her mother had pushed, wanting her daughter to have a future that involved grandbabies rather than regulators, but Lillian had been surprisingly firm. That was a bit unusual for her; standing up to her mother wasn't something she normally did. Maybe that was just another result of the transformative power of scuba diving.

Pamela breezed into the office door at exactly 10:20 a.m., an hour after the other partners. She was smiling, not a polite 'good morning' smile, but an ear-to-ear, 'I've got big news to share' grin.

It took exactly one minute for Lillian's boss to approach her desk and find a reason to flash the large ring decorating her left hand. At least three carats, the sparkling, princess-cut diamond was encased in an intricate platinum setting that seemed to naturally wrap around Pamela's long elegant finger. Lillian's heart did an unstoppable freefall into her stomach, where it was cushioned by roiling digestive juices as it started to dissolve into nothing. This was almost too much.

Lillian had a choice to make—recognize the ring and attempt a congratulation that didn't sound forced or ignore the ring and attempt a morning greeting.

"Hi, Pamela, isn't the weather nice today?" Lillian focused her eyes downward now, away from the glittering awful ring, and concentrated on finishing up the paperwork she'd been working on before her boss had shown up to ruin an otherwise brilliant Thursday morning. She was proud of herself; her voice didn't quaver, her words sounded almost chipper, only a little forced.

By the tone of Pamela's reply, Lillian could tell her boss had been hoping for an emotional response. "It's a bit cool for my tastes." A pregnant pause, weighted by the news Pamela was dying to birth. "Melvin proposed last night." The rush of words fell flat, the moment successfully ruined by Lillian's refusal to play along with Pamela's cruelty.

Lillian's grip tightened around the black fountain pen she held; her mind imagined the ink-stained point sinking into Pamela's too-perfect face. She wanted to lose control…badly; instead she set the pen gently down on her desk and looked up at her boss. Then something transformative happened.

Suddenly, her heart was back in its proper place, firmly in her chest, pattering away. She'd come to a quick and vivid realization: Mel couldn't hurt her anymore, not past this moment. The cycle of contempt for her feelings was complete; the ring had officially ended the story of Lillian and Mel.

"That's wonderful, Pamela. I'm so happy for you both." Lillian was smiling now, her face displaying the sudden change in her heart's position.

Pamela…was not smiling. "Oh…thank you." Turning quickly and almost spilling the pricey cup of coffee she held, Pamela went into her office and closed the door with a soft click that spoke volumes.

The rest of the day went quickly and, as Lillian readied herself to leave the office, she realized that she didn't want to come back to Stein, Green & Lord ever again—not to the oak desk, the squeaky rolling chair, the piles of files, not to Pamela and Mel's happily-ever-after. The old Lillian would have given the professional two weeks' notice, but this Lillian, forever changed by the freedom of diving and the sparkling of a diamond, did not. She typed up a letter on the firm's business head; it was short, sweet and to the final point.

Pamela was still in her office; she'd only come out once all day—to meet the delivery man from *Guido's*. She hadn't spoken to Lillian and Lillian had nearly laughed when she'd caught a whiff of the food her boss had ordered—it was the very distinct smell of the Western Burger, no mistaking the telltale mix of grilled onions, smoked bacon and the restaurant's signature barbeque sauce. It was Mel's favorite.

That burger, more than anything else, made slipping the sealed envelope containing her resignation letter under Pamela's door easy-peasy and absolutely guilt free.

◊ ◊ ◊ ◊

Lillian woke up before her alarm went off the next morning. She always did that on Fridays, her body knowing it was the end of the work week, her mind ready for a restful two days.

She hadn't really needed to wake up early this Friday though. She'd soaked her dive gear the night before, ensuring any remaining trace of chlorinated water was eliminated, and then put everything up properly to dry. The guest bath had a nice-sized closet; she used to store towels and toilet paper there, but now it was painted dark and used to store her scuba equipment. It would only take her a few moments to pack all of that up and the other trip necessities—clothing, toiletries, tent and snack supplies— were already in her van.

Having over two hours before she had to meet Bernie's group at Midwest Scuba, Lillian steeped a cup of tea and watched the neighbors across the alley as they went about their morning ritual. The husband always sat at the table, talking with the kids and fiddling with his tablet, while the wife bustled about the kitchen making breakfast. Over the years, Lillian had made up names for all the family members, even the dog—she called him Bandit, because he was always sneaking bits of food off the table when no one was paying attention.

On this morning, Lillian was able to watch the family longer than normal. The result was a depressing one. The family members filtered out one by one, leaving to conquer their lives outside the apartment, until only the mother remained and, before tackling the dirty dishes and laundry, the woman sat down at the kitchen table and cried. Lillian turned away from the scene, wanting to give the mother privacy, but she was left with the lucid after-impression of a life defined by marriage and children at the expense of youthful dreams and self-identity.

◊ ◊ ◊ ◊

Everyone but Lillian had chosen to ride in the Midwest Scuba travel bus; she'd opted out, wanting the comfort of her van and to finish the book on CD she'd borrowed from the library last week. She was driving behind the white and red bus now, traveling on I-57 South—a blissful, thoughtless stretch of 175 miles. Her mind was able to concentrate on the story and not worry about missing a turn…not worry about anything really.

For well over two hours, Lillian lived inside the story playing through her speakers; she vividly felt the main character's fear, prayed for the hero to appear and save the day.

The main character had one hand free of her bonds and was fighting her kidnapper, trying to scream, but her voice was too hoarse and weak from dehydration. She'd been gagged and chained in the basement of her own house for three days, never being able to see her assailant, the light always kept dim, his face always kept in shadow. She knew death was near…she knew the end was coming.

The main character didn't know what day it was…Lillian knew though, knew that the main character's father was coming home from his business trip and knew that he was expecting to find his seventeen-year-old daughter safe and sound, his cell phone full of reassuring text messages from his responsible, smart child. As Lillian exited the interstate, she inserted the book's last CD. Mermaid Springs was only twenty-five miles off now, according to the directions she'd printed the night before. She mentally urged the book's reader to hurry; she wanted to know the ending before starting the weekend's adventure.

Less than a half hour later, Lillian pulled into the Mermaid Springs campground and parked her van; her display read that the book had ten minutes left. *The father's cab was pulling up to the house… the daughter was crying… the kidnapper gripped a knife as his free hand reached toward the string hanging from the ceiling that was connected to the basement's single light bulb, ready to reveal his identity to his victim.* Letting the car idle, Lillian listened intently, holding her breath for the climax. She was so engrossed, that she didn't see the person approaching in her side mirror.

Knock, knock.

Lillian jumped, her butt lifting several inches away from the driver's seat and her hand flying to her mouth in surprise. Embarrassed, she quickly clicked off the radio and looked at the person standing next to her vehicle.

"Hey, come on. I'll show you where to set up your tent." Bernie was peering at her through the glass, his eyes shielded from the afternoon sun by a Blackhawks baseball cap. He seemed oblivious to the fact that he'd just scared the pants off his client.

Reluctantly, Lillian turned off the car and opened the door slowly so Bernie had time to move. She knew that the end of the book would haunt her over the weekend. She wanted to know who the kidnapper was; the desire was urgent, like it was her own life in the balance, not the fictional teenage daughter's. All Lillian could think about was the knife in the kidnapper's hand, the light about to illuminate his face. "Should I bring my stuff?"

"Nah. We're going to have lunch before getting started." With that, Bernie headed back toward the rest of the group gathered around the registration hut. Lillian followed, making a mental note that the bathrooms and showers were next to the check-in building and quickly counting her companions. There were ten people. Five paired-up couples and little ole Lillian. Three young guys wearing Midwest Scuba shirts were grabbing gear from the bus' rear storage compartment and putting it on the ground. They all looked to be in their early twenties, maybe on summer break from university.

After paying for the group's camping sites for the weekend, Bernie led everyone over to a large cleared area within seeing distance of the training pavilions and the primary dock. "This is where we'll bunk down for the weekend." As Bernie was talking, the Midwest Scuba guys hauled several large coolers into the clearing. "We aren't going to dive today, but after everyone's set up their tents and gotten cozy, we'll head over to the training pavilions and do a skills-check. Some of you are out of practice and some of you are pretty new to diving. The whole purpose of this trip is to refresh you on proper technique and dive safety."

Bernie walked over to the coolers and lifted their lids. "Don't worry, we're going to have a lot of fun this weekend, but let's be smart about it. I know I was pretty clear about my no alcohol policy on dive trips. If I find you drinking, you won't be diving this weekend and you won't get a refund. On that note," he pulled out several bottles of sports water and started tossing them to people, "stay hydrated and remember that what you eat affects how you dive. You're more than welcome to eat foods you've brought, but I recommend sticking to complex carbs, fruits and proteins. We do provide meals as part of your package and the boys will be bringing around sandwiches and fruit in a minute. We'll do some proper cooking tonight, but nothing beats peanut butter and bread in my book."

Lillian didn't mind peanut butter sandwiches, but preferred them with a bit of jelly. Without the fruity spread, the sandwich seemed to adhere to the roof of her mouth and stay there, despite how much water she drank or how vigorously she worked her tongue. Between too-sticky bites, Lillian got to know some of her trip companions better. Leslie was the school teacher from Springfield; Greg was the waiter with dimples; Nicole was the college student with pink highlights and Aidan was the blonde with brown eyes that Lillian hoped was single. She learned the names of the rest of the group members, but didn't have time to discover much else.

While everyone was getting organized, setting up tents and hauling their gear over to the training pavilions, Lillian noted with pleasure that Aiden was paired up with another guy and not a pretty girlfriend. She was relatively sure that the other guy's name was Ray. The duo seemed chummy, a bit touchy-feely really, and, after Ray stole a quick kiss, Lillian realized that Aiden didn't have a pretty girlfriend, he had a handsome boyfriend. *Probably for the best,* she thought, *this trip is about diving, not man-hunting.* With a grin, Lillian thought about her mom and how much she'd love it if her daughter went for a weekend of diving and brought home a good-looking stud, forgetting all the nonsense about diving and independence. Lillian quickly sobered though…remembering the mother across the alley, crying alone.

◊ ◊ ◊ ◊

Bernie was a very competent instructor, making the rounds to each counter-high practice table. Lillian was at a table by herself, which was a little depressing, a mirror to her current relationship status. At each corner of the training pavilion the Midwest Scuba group was working in, was a two foot spigot rising from the ground. Lillian made her way over to the one nearest her table and soaked the tank straps of her buoyancy vest so they'd stretch nicely around the tank cylinder. Bernie's voice was an audio track to her actions.

"Make sure to soak the BCD tank straps thoroughly and position your tank so that the valve opening is oriented toward you, then slide the straps down over the tank until the top of the BCD is aligned with the top of the tank valve. Too low and you're likely to bang your head on the setup. Make sure the straps are straight and parallel to the ground then tighten them down, snapping the buckles closed." Bernie paused, walking over to Leslie the school teacher and lifting her dive vest; as he did, the tank slipped and fell several inches toward the table. "If you aren't physically able to tighten down the straps securely, ask your dive buddy for help. That's why we pair up—for support and safety." On Bernie's cue, Leslie's partner, a tall brunette woman named Carrie, came over and secured the straps firmly while Leslie held the tank upright.

"Remove the dust cap and attach your first stage now; orient the knob away from your body with the second stage and octopus positioned on your left side with computer gauges on your right. Now, attach the low pressure hose to the low inflator valve of your BCD. You should hear a click if the connector attaches properly." Bernie kept talking and Lillian let his voice lull into a dull hum as she put her gear together mechanically. She felt like an old hand at it now, so many mornings spent practicing at the aquatic center. When she'd finished, Lillian turned the valve knob counter-clockwise and watched the pressure gauge's needle rise steadily until it settled just shy of a full tank of air. She looked around at the rest of the group. Most were finished, but Leslie and Carrie were being assisted by one of the Midwest Scuba staff. It looked like Leslie had her first stage oriented backwards, the valve not lined up properly.

When everyone had their dive gear assembled properly, Bernie had them break down the equipment and start the process again. Lillian finished quickly and then double-checked the setup to make sure she hadn't made an error— she hadn't. It was approaching dusk now, the sun skimming the horizon and peeking through the tree line.

On the lakeshore, one group of divers was exiting the lake while another prepared to enter the water for an evening dive. Lillian was looking forward to taking more dive courses—night diving, enriched air, underwater photography. It was *such* a world to explore.

"Alright, does everyone feel comfortable?" Bernie made sure everyone flashed the okay sign before moving onto dive tables, practical theory and safety. The group stayed in the training pavilion until well after dark; fluorescent lights gave the woods an eerie appearance. The hazel water of the lake was illuminated, underwater lights outlining the submerged training platforms.

As the Midwest Scuba group headed back to their camp, Lillian saw the night divers emerge from the placid lake, the lights on their dive masks bobbing about like drunken fireflies floating above the wetness.

Dinner was simple but delicious—cubes of chicken, quartered onions and thickly sliced peppers grilled over the fire pits on skewers, smoked ears of corn slathered in butter, and soft, warm biscuits. Slices of watermelon followed for dessert. The talk was excited, everyone feeling ready after the intensive re-training session. Lillian ate slowly, finishing long after the rest of the group. She was the last to throw away her plate, the last to head toward the facilities to use the restroom and brush her teeth.

The bathrooms were very nice and it was easy to tell that they were consistently maintained. After relieving herself, Lillian brushed her hair back into a long ponytail and wetted her face. Her small, purple toiletry bag was perched on the thin rim of the small sink. She examined her face in the mirror for a while, noting new wrinkles and signs of age. She still wore the silver mermaid earrings. Normally, she'd take all her jewelry off for bed, but this night, something made her keep them on, the dangling fish-women reminders of who she was inside.

Taking out her almond face scrub, Lillian squeezed some onto her fingers and began to work the thick paste into her skin. She loved the feel of it, gritty and course, like it would take a layer of delicate skin off with the dirt and grime of the day. The cool water she splashed onto her face next rinsed away more than the almond cleanser and day's filth. She brushed her teeth next and then applied a new coat of flowery deodorant. Part of her wanted to take a shower, but figured it would be pointless, considering she'd be soaked with lake water the next morning.

Feeling refreshed, Lillian made her way back to camp. She took her time, choosing to detour and walk the lakeshore for a while. It was chilly, but beautiful beside the water; the blue-green seemed to glow with an etherealness that couldn't possibly be produced by the artificial lights above and beneath the lake's surface. The sight made her stay longer than she intended, made her walk onto the longest dock and head toward its furthermost end, at least 65 feet out onto the beautiful lake.

She sat cross-legged on the end of the dock now, enjoying the night and the stars, made barely visible by the ambient light traveling skyward from Mermaid Springs. Her mind wandered here and there, finally settling on the van and the unfinished book sitting in the disc player. The dive training and socializing had pushed it from her mind, but now it was back, front and center, and the desire to hear the end, to put that story to rest, was palpable.

Behind her, the campground lights flashed, signaling the close of dive time for the day. Lillian didn't see anyone else in the water though and no telltale bubbles of air hitting the lake surface. No, everyone had left the hazel water for the night, sensibly resting for the next day.

Lillian knew that she too should head back to her tent, cozy down in her thin sleeping bag and lay her head on her lumpy pillow. All the dive training in the world meant nothing if she weren't well-rested. Standing, she stretched, putting her hands on her hips and bending her upper half backwards until she heard a satisfying series of vertebrae pops.

She didn't immediately start walking away from the water though. After the campground lights had flashed, they'd dimmed; her eyes had adjusted to the lower light and could now see the opposite lakeshore in shadows and contours, trees and outcroppings of rock.

Something was moving in the water near that opposite shore, bobbing up and down. At first, Lillian thought it was a large log, moving naturally in the water… but what was making it move? There was no breeze, no movement-inducing wind. The lake surface was like dark green glass now, perfectly still and serene.

Leaning forward, her body now partway over the water below, she squinted, trying to see the object moving on the other side of the lake.

But it wasn't on the other side of the lake now; it was moving forward, moving toward her. Startled, Lillian tried to move back quickly, but the thong strap on the sandal between the toes on her right foot slipped. In her effort to keep the shoe on her foot, Lillian shoved her foot forward while still trying to move backward. The two actions were not reconcilable, destabilizing her footing. She should have fallen backwards and landed on the dock, but instead, her body, in some subconscious bid to overcorrect, fell forward…into the water, into the path of whatever was moving toward her side of the lake.

It is the natural human reaction to panic, to thrash about wildly in the face of oncoming peril. Lillian was the picture of human reaction now as she pushed to the surface, gasped for air and frantically whirled from facing the rust-red and white dock to stare out into the body of water.

Raising her left hand, she wiped at her eyes, trying to clear them of the mineral-rich wetness. The thing was still moving through the water. It was halfway across the lake now. She couldn't make out any details…not yet. Hyperventilating now, Lillian turned back around and gripped the dock; she tried to pull herself up, but lacked the upper body strength. A few feet to her left, were a set of stairs for divers to access the submerged training platforms. Lillian pushed away from the dock, kicking in earnest to reach those stairs before the unknown creature in the water reached her.

Reaching the stairs, Lillian ducked under the steel railing and scrambled up the wet, partially submerged steps. When she was fully out of the water, she ran the length of the dock and didn't turn back to look until her feet were on land. She'd lost both of her sandals in the water, but she didn't care. Her eyes scanned the water, confusion filled her mind. The lake was still, as serene as ever, the dark surface looked like a mirror. Had she imagined the movement in the water? She waited several minutes, wanting to be sure. There was nothing. Just a peaceful lake tainted by an overactive imagination…but still.

Lillian made her way back to her group's encampment, tentatively waving at Bernie and several of her companions still chatting by the dying cooking fire before entering her two-person tent. She tried to make herself comfortable- changing into dry clothes, sliding down into her sleeping bag and plumping her lumpy pillow several times, but, in the end, she knew she wouldn't get a wink of sleep with only the thin tent material protecting her from the world outside.

She waited until her companions had all gone to sleep and then Lillian sheepishly snuck out of her tent and fast-walked to her car, using her pillow as a pitiful body shield. She didn't even finish her book on CD, her nerves too frayed to listen to a horror story that might ignite a fantastical picture of the unseen creature living in the hazel water of Mermaid Springs.

◊ ◊ ◊ ◊

Waking up at first light, Lillian's body ached from sleeping upright. She'd been leaning up against the driver's door, her pillow tucked beneath her cheek. She must have slept hard, because the pillow was damp with drool, but her brain felt like she hadn't slept at all; she'd had the worst sort of dreams last night, the kind that are impossibly vivid and gut-wrenchingly real. She didn't feel physically or mentally rested—which wasn't a good thing right before a dive.

The left side of her face felt funny, like something had been pushing into the skin all night. Rubbing her cheek, Lillian remembered she'd left on her mermaid earrings. She took them out, one by one, and set them on the van's dash. They glinted dully there, like their luster had faded overnight.

Only Bernie and his staff were up when Lillian dragged herself back to camp. No one said a word about her disheveled appearance as she sat down on one of the large logs circled around the fire pit. "Morning."

"Morning to you. Rough night?" Bernie poured a cup of coffee from a steel kettle resting in the hot coals at the edge of the morning fire.

"A bit." Lillian took the blue-speckled mug Bernie offered her. "Thanks."

"Okay to dive?"

Lillian was quiet for a minute. *Did she want to dive? Did she want to go back into the water?* She glanced at her tent, thinking about the lake-water-soaked clothes that likely smelled of mildew now, having sat overnight in a twisted heap. Lillian realized the real question was: *Was she willing to give up diving, an activity that had helped her reclaim her sense of self-worth, over a silly hallucination?* "Yep. I'm definitely okay. Besides, you're my partner; I'll be safe as can be."

The older man chuckled and nodded. "Yes ma'am. I'll keep you safe as houses."

She had no idea what that meant, but had every faith that Bernie would keep her on her toes during the two planned dives. The first was a group dive, a gradual descent to the second deepest submerged platform at 85 feet, with skills tests on the platforms at 20 and 60 feet. The dive instructor had walked the group through what would happen while at the training pavilion yesterday. The focus would be on equalization during descent, adjusting buoyancy, buddy breathing and a slew of other techniques to ensure underwater survival. The second dive though, that would be freedom. Well, it would be supervised freedom.

Breakfast was light, premixed protein shakes and fruit, and Bernie held a vote to decide the location for the exploration dive. The group elected to check out the submerged Boeing 727 and surrounding area. There was a lot sunken in that section of the lake—an ambulance, a fire truck, a coal car. Thinking about all the things Lillian would see underwater, the scary experience by the lake started to sink into distant, obscure memory. The group wouldn't have time to see everything in one shot, but Bernie had offered to do an early morning dive with anyone who wanted a little more exploring time before heading home. The filling station was convenient to the camp. Lillian planned to be first in line to refill her dive tank for the morning.

◊ ◊ ◊ ◊

The day was flying by and Lillian was having a wonderful time. Two of Bernie's staff had buddied up for the skills dive and helped everyone along. On the submerged platform at twenty feet, Bernie had instructed everyone to take their regulators out of their mouths and let them float away. Lilian had retrieved her second stage smoothly, rolling her left shoulder down as she moved her arm backwards, bending her elbow and catching the regulator hose with the crook of her arm. Leslie had a bit of trouble though; she seemed to be the problematic student on the trip.

Lunch was over now, the sun well past noon in the sky and the group was prepping for the exploration dive. It was a shore dive and everyone's equipment was assembled and resting on large gray tarps on the ground. Lillian was zipping up her wetsuit, the black and blue material like a second skin against her body; it was still slightly wet from the skills dive and felt a bit squishy.

"Alright, grab your buddies. It's go time." Bernie called. "It will be easier for most of you to inflate your BCD and carry your gear into the water. Make sure your buddy checks your setup and we'll circle up and start the descent together. Remember, if you lose your buddy, make a slow ascent with safety stops and surface." Leaving his staff to assist the rest of the group, Bernie walked toward Lillian, his face breaking into a wide grin.

Lillian was surprised by the exaggerated grin; it made the man's face transform appealingly, somehow make him a little more than 'okay' looking and decidedly youthful. *Stop it!* Lillian mentally berated herself; *He's way too old and this trip is NOT about men; it's about me and being strong and independent.* With that subvocalized yell, she got her head in the game and off the tiny dimples that appeared on Bernie's chin when he smiled widely. *I'm totally hopeless.* She thought with chagrin, her mind quickly returning to the dive instructor's chin divots.

In reality, the water felt the same as it had during the morning skill's dive, but, in Lillian's mind, it felt infinitely more welcoming—warmer, wetter, the taste more mineral-rich in her mouth. She and Bernie had performed a shore gear-check before entering the lake. Lillian's vest was inflated and floating by her now while she performed another safety-check on Bernie's set up. "Looks good. Same as it did five minutes ago." She turned from her 'buddy' and began to put on her own equipment. She had to half-float backwards and then angle forward using her upper body strength to regain a solid footing on the lake bed. Putting on her fins wasn't nearly as awkward; Bernie let her lean against him for support. Shore diving was definitely a new experience; at the aquatic center, Lillian always sat on the pool's edge and got ready then butt-scooted into the water.

Scanning the lake, taking it all in, Lillian waited patiently while Bernie checked her setup. The rest of the group was also performing last minute checks, circled up and waiting on the dive master's go ahead to descend. "Alright. You look good." Bernie patted her back and then turned to face the rest of the group. "This is a 40 minute dive; we'll head northeast toward the Boeing, start at its tail and descend to its nose submerged at 50 feet. Some of you will consume your air slower, others faster; regardless, we'll begin our ascent at the 40 minute mark. We may have time to explore the ambulance or fire truck on the way back to shore. This is a group exploration dive, so let's stay pretty close together."

Bernie put on his mask, secured the straps tight around his head and stuck his regulator in his mouth. The group played follow-the-leader, copying his movements. At the 'ok' sign, everyone sank into the shallow water, adjusting the air in their vests to hover above the lake floor. The group did a decent job of staying together; Lillian was on the end with Bernie to her right. Every few leg kicks, he'd flash the 'ok' sign and she'd respond mechanically, her mind on the wetness around her, the sights that were slowly emerging from the green haze.

This is what she'd been waiting for—to sink below the hazel surface of the unassuming lake and see more than pool swimmers through clear chlorinated water or submerged training platforms and the occasional unattractive fish. If she could only scuba dive to eternity, never resurface to deal with the messy world above. She often thought about that, just closing her eyes and become the wetness around her. She wasn't that brave though, not really.

They were at fifteen feet now and passing the Mermaid Springs 'petting zoo,' an eerie assortment of rough-hewn statues seeming to rise out of the lake's bottom. It wasn't quaint and cheery...it was disturbing.

Lillian's eyes focused on a long animal; it was odd looking, almost seeming to sway along with the water's movement, but it was stone...and that was a silly notion. Maybe it was supposed to be a sea serpent? But the body, though long and curved, was also twisted and nodular, too thick to be a snake. Lillian's mask was fogging a bit; she'd scrubbed it with toothpaste the night before and swished spit on the lenses before hitting the water, but it was fogging nonetheless. She tapped Bernie's shoulder and when he looked, she pointed at her mask. He gave her the okay sign and mocked lifting his own mask slightly to allow water entry, reminding her how to eliminate the fog.

Coming to a stop and orienting herself to float upright, Lillian gripped the mask's rubber skirt above her right eyebrow and barely broke the seal between mask and skin. She let water trickle in until it was at eye level then tilted her head back and pushed the top of the mask into her forehead firmly. Taking a deep drag from the second stage, she exhaled through her nose forcefully, like she had a beef with a particularly stubborn booger. She had to do it twice before her mask was fog and water-free. It only took a minute, but Lillian felt bad when she looked around and realized Bernie had signaled the whole group to wait on her.

As the group began to swim forward, Lillian looked over at the odd serpent shape in the rock zoo, but…it wasn't there. Where it had been, between inanimate skunk and motionless rabbit, was just an empty space of murky jade. Lillian dismissed this, thinking that the fogging of her mask had tricked her eyes.

◊ ◊ ◊ ◊

The group was at 50 feet, exploring the nose of the sunken plane. It was hollow, all glass and doors removed so divers could enter and exit at various points.

Lillian and Bernie were separated by a space of four feet; his eyes were scanning the rest of the group, making sure everyone was okay and Lillian's eyes were focused elsewhere, her head tilted back so she could look up the length of the plane to the tail, resting at fifteen feet below the lake's surface. The water was brighter there, the afternoon light less filtered. A long, serpent-like form peeked from behind the plane's broken rudder. Lilian blinked, almost rubbed her mask lenses with a gloved finger, but stopped herself, realizing that there was no fog to wipe away.

Subconsciously, Lillian moved, kicking her legs slowly, the fins displacing water and propelling her upward to satisfy morbid curiosity. She gave no thought to safety stops as she ascended, her mind solely concentrated on solving the mystery of the thick, tentacle like shape haunting the hazel lake. She was still scared, the feeling pulsating throughout her body, but nothing would keep her from her determined course.

When Bernie turned from the group to check on his buddy, he found only the area she once occupied. He whirled, looking about and then paused, intuition leading his eyes to the watery space above. She was kicking toward the surface, ten feet above him. How had he not felt the movement, the push of pressure against his back as his partner moved toward the surface? She wasn't pausing, not stopping to let her body equalize and eliminate nitrogen. Eyes wide, the seasoned instructor turned back to the group and gave them the signal to ascend with stops. Everyone looked confused, not understanding why the exploration dive was being cut short, but they followed instructions, moving away from the Boeing and beginning the slow path to surface.

When the others had risen fifteen feet and paused for a safety stop, Bernie turned to follow Lillian. He didn't see her now though. She was out of his line of sight, maybe around the other side of the plane, hidden from view. *She's gonna get the damn bends.* Bernie was pissed and worried. He hadn't had a client get hurt on a dive in over a decade; he wasn't aiming to break that record today. He took his time, too practiced to risk health in his rush to find Lillian. He paused at 30 feet, taking a 3 minute safety and scanning the space above for his dive buddy. Still no sign of her.

◊ ◊ ◊ ◊

Lillian was being pulled through the water at breakneck speed. Every now and then, she caught a quick glimpse of large, seal-like flappers rotating forward and backward in a repetitive motion that seemed impossibly swift. Each fin was crowned in five misshapen digits... like the left overs of evolution, vestigial fingers no longer required for thriving in an aquatic environment.

The mystery tentacle was wrapped around her middle, squeezing her tightly. It wasn't a tentacle though; it was a malformed, knobby tail covered in dark scales that glinted dully in the filtered light traveling through the jade water. Where the glassy scales were not, stained lengths of ivory protruded in knotty, misshapen masses. It looked as if two saplings had grown too close together, wrapping around each other in a lopsided braid, decorated by bits of moss and loose bark.

The end of the tentacle curved upward toward her face now; she was belly-down, oriented toward the lake floor being pulled behind the creature. When it came into view, Lillian screamed involuntarily, her regulator falling from her mouth, sending a jet of air into the water. Toes. Twisted, broken toes grown together in a huddled mass. And the 'tail' wrapped around her body was...legs...fused together and twisted in an unnatural, horrific way. And the digits crowning the seal-like flappers were fingers, human vestigial fingers...

Bile rose in Lillian's esophagus, yellow vomit streamed out of her mouth and trailed behind her as the thing that once was human dragged her into the dark abyss, into the small cavern mouth in the bottom of the lake bed. And, even though she'd often fantasized about an eternal rest below the water, to say goodbye to life's problems and find peace, Lillian's heart raced and her unheard voice prayed for rescue.

◊ ◊ ◊ ◊

The creature was male; there was no denying that, the telltale appendage hanging loosely in front of the twisted legs a constant reminder. It was almost funny to Lillian, her body bound by wet, semi-decayed rope and uncomfortably stuffed on a rocky, wide ledge inside the damp cavern—a man had interfered with her weekend after all. A nightmarish mermaid—nothing like the singing, joyful, beautiful creatures in movies.

There was nothing funny about the situation though, nothing chuckle-worthy and humorous, even in the darkest sense.

The creature's… *his*…upper body was as malformed as his lower. His forearms scaled and winged, his face almost melted, the eyes resting astride the nose, the nose curving downward to graze the lower, nearly nonexistent lip.

He stared at her from his perch on the other side of the small pool where the watery tunnel terminated. He lowered himself back into the water and began to move closer to her, spittle gathering at the corners of his mouth. The intent in his eyes was clear, clear even to a woman whose relationship history was spotted with failure after failure. He had not bound her mouth; no one would hear her scream for help.

As he used his gnarled fingers to unzip Lillian's black and cobalt wetsuit, he rose higher in the water, revealing intent incarnate; his body grown hard with anticipation. Untying the cords around her lower body, he positioned himself on top of her. Lillian wiggled in protest, trying to keep her legs closed, her womanhood protected, but his upper body was too strong. His arms—so used to cleaving through the water—easily forced her thighs apart. And, although no one could possibly hear her, Lillian screamed as he entered.

His movements were like a dying fish, flapping about on the deck of a boat. In and out. In and out. He arched upward and thrust forward, his twisted fin hitting the inside of Lillian's thighs and making a sickeningly wet sound. It felt like snakeskin, rubbing against her. She tried not to scream again. She tried not to whimper, but every few thrusts, Lillian involuntarily sobbed, her whole body vibrating. This movement, this sound, only seemed to increase her assailant's fervor.

She tried to go elsewhere in her mind; see a happier time and forget the pain of the moment, but there were no pretty pictures in her brain. Only thoughts of the recent months, the recent happenings in her life; thoughts of Mel, Pamela, her mother, her sister…thoughts of the crying woman living next door and the book in her van's CD player, the ending of which she'd never know.

Unable to deal with the feel of his body against hers, the sound of his satisfaction as he fertilized her womb, Lillian drifted off into nothingness.

◊ ◊ ◊ ◊

"We've searched the lake twice, Bernie. She's not here. Maybe she surfaced and left."

"Her van's still here, Leon. It's unlocked and all her stuff is in her tent. She didn't leave and she didn't vanish. Are you sure we've checked everywhere? We should check the plane again or the ambulance. She's got to be somewhere." The dive instructor rubbed his eyes, exhausted from hours of endless searching. "She can't have disappeared." He mumbled, resting his face in one hand for a defeated moment. His other hand was formed in a tight fist.

"Sure, Bernie. We'll keep looking. Cops are sending people to search too."

Looking every day his 65 years, Bernie walked away from Leon and headed to the longest dock. He walked to the very edge. His gaze took in the whole expanse of Mermaid Springs Lake. The hazel water did not look so attractive now, not with the mystery of Lillian's disappearance hovering over the beauty. He lifted his fisted hand and opened it slowly, revealing earrings. The dull silver mermaids seemed to taunt Bernie. Anger flashed within him and he threw with all his might. The small pieces of formed metal made an almost soundless whisper as they entered the water.

It was after nightfall and behind Bernie, the campground lights flashed and dimmed. His eyes adjusted quickly; beneath the water, the lights trimming the submerged training platforms shone dimly. He could barely see the distant shore now.

Movement, splashing across the lake. Something in the water...two somethings. Moving toward the dock where Bernie stood.

IN CHICAGO, THE DISH IS SO DEEP, NO ONE CAN HEAR YOU SCREAM
by Frank J. Edler

H ave you heard of the haunted deep dish pizza of Chicago?

No?

I didn't think so, I'd love to tell you about it. Go on, have a seat. This won't take long I promise but it's important to know where you're coming from before you know where you're heading. It could mean life or death in Chicago, especially if you're in the mood for one of Chicago's famous deep dish pizzas.

I know that's exactly the position I found myself in when I came face to face with Chicago's Haunted Deep Dish. I should have known better too, I am a ghost hunter after all. Perhaps you remember me? They call me Spook, host of *Spooked*, the reality TV show on that cable channel. I visited haunted places around the country, trying to prove beyond the shadow of a doubt that ghosts exist while obtaining irrefutable evidence to back up my claims.

Nothing? I can understand. I mean, I was just one ghost hunter in a sea of ghost hunting reality shows that saturated the reality TV market. It's easy to not get noticed when the parade of shows start to become cookie cutter versions of one another, each more hack than the other. Of course, there was the abrupt cancellation of my show, but let's not get into that right now.

I'll let you in on a little secret though, because I'm in a position where I can; not only is my show a bunch of bullshit, they all are. Yup! Not one ghost hunting show on TV is reality based. The ugly truth is we twist the meaning of 'real' and the public doesn't care as long as they want to believe. You don't have to convince those idiots of anything, they're already sold!

I'm not even ashamed of it. Why should I be? Perhaps you haven't heard of me or my show, that's okay. I still got paid by some second rate, basic cable channel. There must have been an audience somewhere for them to throw the kind of money at me that they did. Fame wasn't the name of the game though.

I did have a thriving paranormal investigation business before the TV gig. I had all types of electronic equipment. There was stuff for detecting sound waves that humans couldn't hear, laser thermal scanners for detecting cold or hot spots. Of course the electromagnetic pulse meters for seeking out anomalies in the magnetic fields of the locations I was investigating. All manner of funky scientific toys to legitimize what was also a business of smoke and mirrors. Yeah, I don't need TV cameras around to play the game of bullshitting people into thinking ghosts exist. I'm not a ghost hunter, I'm a con artist.

At least that's what I had myself believe before I got conned by my own con. I wound up here in Chicago, hunting down a local haunt for the TV show. It wasn't even the haunted deep dish I'm in Chicago for now. Rather, we were filming for an episode of *Spooked* about the famous Chicago area legend of Resurrection Mary.

I'm sure you've heard of her, she been around longer then I have and she's maybe one of the most famous ghost stories in the Chicago area. Mary was at a dance, some time ago, with her boyfriend. They got into an argument one bitter cold Chicago evening and she stormed out of the dance hall. She walked along a nearby road, very late at night, hitchhiking for a ride home. She was struck and killed by a motorist who didn't see her in the dark. The car drove off, leaving her for dead. Her parents buried her body, clad in a flowing white dress and matching white shoes in Resurrection Cemetery. Since then many motorists driving in the area of Resurrection Cemetery have seen her hitchhiking along the side of the road near the cemetery. In some cases, people have even claimed to have picked her up only to find out they have a specter in their car. There are, of course, many variations to the story; there always are, all bone-chilling despite the fact that I find ghost stories to be balderdash.

Anyway, my crew was able to put together a nice show on the ghost. We hired a local talent to play Mary dressed in her flowing white dress. We interviewed several people who claimed to have had run-ins with Resurrection Mary. I played with my gadgets, making them blip, blink and whir for the cameras. Later, when it's edited together it will look exactly as if we had our own run in with the ghost of Resurrection Mary. No one will be the wiser, not even those who helped take part in the shoot.

So, after a successful wrap up in shooting, I drove back to Chicago where the network put me up in a nice hotel. I ask the hotel staff for recommendations of places to go eat. Just my luck too, one of the bell-hops was a fan of the show and of Chicago urban legends. He told me he knew the perfect place for me to go have dinner that night.

It's a place called "La Cucina Dei Dannati", it sounded like a restaurant straight out of Naples. There is nothing I dislike more than Italian food chain restaurants. If you've ever had good, authentic, homemade Italian food you'll understand exactly what I'm talking about. The bellboy told me it was a quaint little place with an atmosphere I would enjoy and that their deep dish pizza was to die for. He gave me directions, noting it was a tricky little place to spot from the street, but located in the Little Italy section of Chicago, which only helped solidify my decision to go.

I took a cab and just as the bell-hop had promised, the address was tricky to find. Neither me nor the cab driver could figure it out from the cab. I had him drop me off about where the restaurant should be and paid him then sent him on his merry way.

I looked again at the address written on a torn piece of paper the bellboy gave me back at the hotel. 1366 West Taylor Street. Several brick buildings lined the street, each with a shop on the first floor and apartments above, like you would find in most big cities. There was 1364 to my right, Gallucci's Real Estate Agency. Then an alley between the buildings. The next number was 1368, the location of Vince's Barber Shop. An old fashioned red and white barber pole twirled away out front.

The missing building perplexed me, but I kept focusing on the dark alley space between the two brick structures and heard the bellboy in my head telling me the restaurant was tricky to find from the street. I gambled on finding La Cucina Dei Dannati down the narrow alleyway.

I deal with ghosts almost every day. My work has put me in some creepy places. Abandoned asylums, dark cemeteries and creaky old houses are all part of the job. None of them ever made my spine tingle, even in the most spine-tingling of situations. I know what I do is malarkey, there's nothing scary about that.

I can tell you though, I was completely taken off guard when I entered the space between those two buildings. Ice shot through my spine and crystallized throughout every nerve ending in my body. It was a breathtaking moment and I thought I was going to drop dead of a heart attack with the sudden and unexpected sensation. It was not in my nature to equate that to anything paranormal so I never thought anymore of it then, I should have.

I caught my breath and regained my composure and walked further into the alley. The smell of sweet roasting garlic and stewing tomatoes on the air relieved me as I walked further on. There was definitely someone back here cooking some great smelling Italian food. My mouth started to salivate, it smelled so good.

The two buildings towering over me on either side created a spooky twilight in the early evening. Several dozen paces down, the alley opened up into a small court with an inviting little wooden door at the back. A hand painted wooden sign over the top read, "La Cucina Dei Dannati". I got a sense of what the atmosphere inside would be like from the sign hung above the door. It pictured tomatoes with creepy black hollow faces on them, like something out of Edvard Munch's "The Scream." I chuckled when I saw that and knew exactly why the bellboy had sent me here, an Italian restaurant with a spooky flair. Nice.

I opened the door and it creaked exactly like a spooky old door should. Taking in the view of the inside, I couldn't be sure if that creak was manufactured or natural, either way it lent to the atmosphere. The dining room was small and low lit with seating for maybe twenty or so guests at a time. A large, bizarre mural was painted on the wall which ran the length of the building. It looked like a scene right out of Dante's Inferno, save for some of the Damned serving pizza pies to others. The Damned serving the pizzas looked elated, the Damned eating the pizzas looked horrified, though the difference was subtle.

The ceiling was black with oddities hanging down here

and there; a shrunken head, a wooden hex symbol, and what looked like a mummified cat of some sort. In the corners I could make out stone gargoyles keeping watch from the dark shadows.

A figure seemed to appear from out of nowhere in my peripheral vision.

I jumped, startled by the hostess who appeared at my side. Where did she even come from? There was no hostess stand and I didn't see her there when I walked in. I must have been so taken by the art and trinkets, that I didn't notice her approach.

She was definitely part and parcel with the atmosphere. Her jet black hair teased out like a refugee from the 1980's, a leather corset with a plunging neckline to her navel. She did little to hide her milky-white breasts, dying to burst out of their leather chamber in all their perky glory. Her image screamed 'vampire' right down to her sharp-toothed smile.

"Sir, will you be dining alone this evening?" she asked.

"Yes, just me this evening. Your restaurant was recommended to me by a fan of mine." I flashed my debonair, on-camera smile. I figured anyone working here would definitely watch my show, but the hostess only returned my smile and motioned for me to follow her to my table.

She showed me to a small two-seat table roughly dead center on the Dante's Inferno wall. I sat and she handed me a menu as I unfolded my napkin and placed it in my lap. She assured me my waitress would be along in just a moment and she walked back towards the front door.

I opened the menu to browse the selection and peered back up at the hostess to try to steal a glimpse of her posterior as she sauntered away, but she was already out of sight. I raised my eyebrows, astonished that she seemed to have disappeared as fast as she appeared.

Before I had a chance to take a good look at the menu, my waitress did indeed come to greet me. Immediately she struck me as a female Beetlejuice, clad in black and white striped pants and shirt. Her face whited out, her mouth painted to look as if it were sewn closed with thick black thread. It must have been a trick of the dim lighting or a good makeup job she had, but when she spoke I could not see her lips moving.

"Good evening, welcome to La Cucina Dei Dannati. My name is Ghoulia, can I get you something to drink?" She said through motionless lips.

I snickered, astonished at the trick, "Yes, I'll have a glass of the house's finest red wine please."

"Excellent, sir. Can I interest you in our specials this evening?"

"Yes, I would love to hear them."

"Chicago Deep Dish Pizza."

I waited a beat for her to go on. She just stood there looking at me.

"Oh. That's the special?"

"Yes, sir."

I was a bit disappointed. I could get a Chicago deep dish in just about any restaurant I walked into in this city. It was a cookie cutter item anywhere you went and almost disappointing as a signature food of the city, it seemed pointless being on the house specials menu.

Still, the decor of the establishment had tickled my fancy and the quirky staff playing out their roles had me sold. I recalled the bellboy tell me it was the thing to eat here also. If La Cucina Dei Dannati was featuring a Chicago Deep Dish tonight then I was going to go along for the ride.

"That's fine. I'll have the deep dish."

"A fine choice, sir" She said through tight lips and

limped away, the gait of a zombie girl. Well played. At this rate, I couldn't wait to meet the chef.

The ghoul waitress brought me my glass of wine. I took a sip and examined the wall mural further. It had wonderful detail for a restaurant painting, the longer I gazed at it the more it seemed to come alive. I became transfixed. I could swear the flames flickered in the brimstone causing the shadows to shimmer in the background.

I blinked hard to break the spell it had me under. I looked at my glass and thought, "damn, that's some good wine."

I picked it up to take another sip. As I brought it to my lips I saw that it was boiling. I freaked and dropped the glass, the wine spilling all over the table and into my lap. I stood fast, anticipating the scalding sensation but it never came. The wine was room temperature as it should be.

"Is everything okay, sir? Oh, you've spilled your wine. I'll get you a new glass and something to clean yourself off with. Here is your pizza." Ghoulia said.

She placed the pizza down on the table. The dish was deep, it could have been the deepest dish I've ever seen a pizza cooked in, three inches at least. The pan itself a heavy, black, cast iron that looked like it had not been used since the dark ages.

"Wow, that was fast!" I said, sitting back down, trying my best to sound cool.

"Fast? If you think twenty minutes is fast, I might take you home with me tonight!" She quipped through closed lips and punctuated it with a wink. "Let me go get you some club soda to get that wine stain out of your pants."

Twenty minutes? I was staring at the wall for twenty minutes? It only felt like a minute or two, five at best if I had zoned, not twenty. The idea left me disoriented, trying to account for the missing time. Was the wine hitting me that hard already? I only had one sip, hadn't I?

I felt so weird though. Was I buzzed off one sip?

"Psst."

I looked around, did someone just try to grab my attention?

"Psst. Right here!"

I looked again. The waitress was off in the kitchen getting my club soda, the hostess was still out of sight, I was the only one in the dining room.

"Psst. Look down Dope."

I looked down at my pizza. It was still throwing off wisps of steam. I hadn't noticed before but the toppings on the pizza created a smiley face. Two pieces of pepperoni for eyes with an anchovy above each for eyebrows, a curved slice of green pepper formed a nose and a bunch of sliced black olives lined up in a row to form a mouth. I thought it was rather cheesy of the chef to treat me like a child by making my pizza cute until the toppings articulated into an animated face.

"Hey Bub," my pizza said to me, "Aren't you the guy on TV?"

Holy fuck, this was some potent wine!

The pizza knew I wasn't believing what I was seeing, "You are, aren't you? You got the shine. Ever see that movie? Good flick, great book."

I wanted to pick up the pan and look underneath for the electronics controlling this talking pizza. There had to have been a special effects hobbyist working here. I touched the side to pick it up and burnt the tips of my fingers. Dang, it was still hot! They did a great job of protecting the electronics inside against such high heat. I had to have this on my show! Haunted pizza, that just beat all!

I called out to the dining room, "Hey this is neat! You can cut the gag now, you don't have me fooled." I looked around, still no hostess and the waitress was still in the back getting the club soda.

I got up to go get her in the kitchen where I figured they had the control room set up anyway.

"Is there a problem, sir?" The vampire hostess asked from behind me as I walked back through the kitchen.

I spun around, startled, "Where the hell did you come from?"

"I've been here the whole time, sir. Is there a problem? What were you just screaming about?"

"Oh, I wasn't screaming. I just was blown away by the animatronic pizza. The whole atmosphere, in truth. Your disappearing act and Ghoulia's ventriloquist routine and now this talking pizza. I gotta feature this place on my TV show. Perhaps you heard of me, they call me Spook, I do the reality show, *Spooked*?"

"I'm not sure what you're talking about, sir." she said, perplexed.

"It's okay, not everyone knows me, I'm only on basic cable. But, I do this show on ghost hunting..."

"Hunting," she asked, "but it is we who have found you. I would say you are the hunted not the hunter."

"I...it's just that...wait, what do you mean you found me? I thought you just said you don't know anything about my show."

"We don't know anything about a television show. Azzip Shidpeed, he of the voracious insatiable appetite beckons his meals. He chose you. You are the sacrifice as Azzip has decreed this cycle."

I was beginning to think this woman was off her rocker and not just doing an act for the restaurant. I decided I would just sit back at my table and go along for the ride now. Before I could, Ghoulia ambushed me from behind and dragged me back to my table. I wanted to protest her manhandling me. The fact is, I was in total shock, I had a hard time wrapping my mind around her superhuman strength and I was back in my seat before I could utter a single word of dissent.

She slammed me back down into my seat and leaned over me, pointing an unnaturally long finger at my face. "Azzip will be having you for dinner. You will sit and enjoy it. Don't make me get forceful with you again!"

Her face was so close to mine by the time she finished yelling at me, our noses almost touched. I could see all too clearly that her lips never parted, not once. I was also unnerved to see it wasn't makeup that made her mouth appear sewn shut. It was sewn closed with what appeared to be leather lacing, old and cracked but still holding strong.

You would think by now I would realize there was something odd going on here. I'm a ghost hunter and I've seen every trick in the book to fool people into believing in the paranormal. The hostess' disappearing trick and Ghoulia's freakish strength, and sealed lips, didn't frighten me at all. To me it demonstrated dedication to the craft, like circus freaks they were willing to go too far for a dollar.

"Yes, ma'am" I said, going along with the act.

Ghoulia shambled back to the kitchen and vampire hostess was already gone. She was getting predictable now.

"You're more feisty than I would have expected. I like that, sure I'm old but I still like an opportunity to play with my food a bit."

The pizza was talking to me again. I would have thought it would be more creepy if it didn't have a trace of Chicago accent in its voice. They needed a better voice actor back there, something a lot more authentic. Maybe a foreigner from an Eastern European country or maybe a washed up B-movie actor, someone who did a poor impersonation of James Earl Jones would have worked.

"I'm prepared to do what is expected of me, Azzip."

"Don't say my name!" the pizza yelled, the steam coming off it intensified for a moment. A blast of heat punctuated its anger.

That caught me off guard.

"I don't want to play with you any longer. It's time for dinner." At that pronouncement, the fires in the mural on the wall burned brighter and bigger. The entire dining room lit up from the raging fires. A speaker system in the ceiling began to play deep mournful music. "Spook, raise the ceremonial dagger and cut into my Earthbound flesh."

I sat there for a moment befuddled by what the pizza was saying. I realized he was asking me to pick up the pizza cutter off the table when his pepperoni eyes furrowed at me.

"Wow, you're good at this," Its voice dripping sarcasm. "Now, slice me, cut into my cheesy flesh, form your triangular shaped wound that your people find most appealing. Cut true and clean, leave no part attached."

It was the most poetic set of instructions I'd ever heard for slicing a pizza. At least, I was pretty sure that's what the pizza was asking of me. I tested the waters.

"Umm, six slices or eight?"

"No!" The pizza said, growing impatient, "One slice of my vessel is all that is necessary, leave the rest unblemished."

I shrugged my shoulders and cut in, crust first then rolled to the center, being certain I cut the whole way through as this lunatic pizza instructed. I rolled back to be sure the cut was clean. Then approximated the size of the slice I wanted and repeated the process again when I was certain the bitchy talking pizza had no objections to the size of the slice.

It didn't.

I repeated the cut, forming a slice fit for a glutton. Truth be told, even though the pizza was talking to me, it still looked delicious.

"Okay Spook, dig in."

I lifted the slice out of the deep dish pan with the spatula Ghoulia brought out alongside of it. Immediately as I lifted the slice out, thick steam rushed out from underneath. Thick, opaque steam enveloped my vision, enveloped the room. It was an impossible amount of steam releasing from under the slice.

The steam didn't scald me whatsoever. It surrounded me, I could not see my hand in front of my face. It grew thicker and thicker, all external light sources drowned out. The room became darker and darker in the thick cloud until everything was black.

Completely dark. Silence, so still I could hear the neurons in my brain firing. Tiny, miniscule crackles within my head.

The steam-fueled cloud dissipated. I think. I can't tell, all I see is black. I can feel my body but I can't hold my hand in front of my face and see it. I feel as if I am still seated at the table, but I felt no chair underneath me. I am suspended in blackness.

I stand up. There is no floor underneath my feet, but I am supported. I take a step forward and move, but go nowhere. There is only a black void that I occupy.

I haven't been here for long, but perhaps I've been here forever. I'm not sure, there is no easy way to know. I've had time to explore the nowhere I inhabit.

I can walk on walls that aren't there, standing at ninety degree angles to where I perceive the floor to be, without ever feeling my spatial frame of reference change. I can do a half-flip and stand on the ceiling that doesn't exist and get the same results.

It's as if I am suspended in black gel. I can move my body and feel as if I'm moving through space but space never moves around me.

I think I'm in the pizza. Or more specifically, the deep dish pan. Perhaps another plane of existence somewhere between Chicago and madness is accurate. I am where the ghosts dwell.

I am a ghost now myself. I know this because the darkness instills it in my psyche, I don't have a brain any longer, at least I don't believe so, I can't see it. But I have a psyche which knows things that the dark tells it.

I like being a ghost. My whole physical life I misled people into believing I didn't exist, I never believed I existed myself. I am a ghost now, a real one. I am my new truth. I like it this way better.

The darkness tells me I can escape this ghostly vessel. I can swap out with another soul and be free. Azzip is everywhere and nowhere and although he trapped me here, it's here where I find I want to be. But, please, don't eat me. I do so love being the Haunted Deep Dish of Chicago.

Please, put down that pizza cutter. Run! Run away now!

CHICAGO BLUES

by Stuart Conover

I t was the first of December and the streets of Chicago were covered in a light gray mist and a spatter of crimson blood. Snow had not yet fallen across the city though the crispness of winter permeated the air. John Wotes stood out on his balcony overlooking the city from forty-two stories up. The smoke he exhaled glowed that light blue usually reserved for those perfect summer nights when the moon was full overhead. Tonight the air was illuminated by the cool glow cast off by the Christmas lights the woman he would always love, had hung all over his balcony. Sirens pierced the air and he coughed. Not the dry cough of a man who has smoked his entire life, but that of a man whose mind was so deep in thought he hadn't noticed he had reached the filter.

The harsh exhale of breath did not distract him as he reached into his pack to light another cigarette. This was a man who had it all 24 hours earlier and now the only thing keeping him from falling apart was to just take another long drag off of the Parliament Lights, which he'd purchased for the first time in over twenty years. It had not yet been a full day since he had gone from a man who had Stacy—the love of his life; a successful career in a research company he had worked years to build from the ground up with his cousin Chris; and a loving group of family and friends.

Now, it was all over. The world was falling apart around him, and all he could do was watch as the smoke slowly grew from the embers and faded into the cloud covered sky.

◊ ◊ ◊ ◊

They had just left a trendy little sushi joint called Osys on Michigan Avenue, usually only a 4 block walk from their condo, but often they would walk through Grand Park on the way home. It was a typical distraction for them; partly an excuse to burn calories; partly an excuse to be out of the house; and mainly an excuse to hold hands while getting away from it all for a few extra minutes. They'd been doing it ever since they saw an old couple taking the time to walk together. After talking to them, they realized taking a little breather from life was clearly something that would help any relationship, even those which were already great—as theirs had been. When they had left, the winter air was barely brisk and it was still almost sunny out. There was a local metal-working artist's work on display in the park that lined the paths.

"It's going to be a white Christmas this year John," she said, "there's always extra snow after a summer like the scorcher that we just had." He couldn't help but laugh at her logic. With Chicago weather, anything could be possible.

It was their weekly date night the couple truly enjoyed doing, and over the past year had become tradition for them. The walk was safe, normal, relaxing. That is, until it wasn't. The strangers had come upon them slow and snarling. At first, they seemed just like teenagers playing around, having a good time.

It was only a moment before they attacked.

Although the men had been moving slowly before, when Stacy neared them they grabbed at her ferociously. Before they could react, one of them bit through her shirt into her shoulder. At first it looked as if they were about to try to rape John's wife, right in front of him, but the one at her shoulder quickly turned to him, blood dripping from his mouth. As pieces of flesh were falling from the madman's lips, John saw red. In his anger, John ripped a heavy metal piece from off of a work of art on display nearby then slammed it into the madman's chest. His eyes were so full of rage, all he could see was the flesh being chewed between the madman's gnashing teeth. The smack of metal against flesh filled the air as he hit the man's chest again. The force of the blow should have dropped a normal man to the ground, but all he did was look up and start moving towards the source of its injury.

In a savage fury John screamed "Leave her alone!" while slamming the twisted metal rod once called art, into the junkie repeatedly. When he finally dropped to the ground, the two others had already fallen upon Stacy, who was lying motionless, whimpering and covered in blood. In a maddening fury, adrenaline pushed John into a killing machine who blindly beat the other attackers, not pausing until they had both stopped moving. The blind rage surging through him, left almost as abruptly as it had come. With the attackers down he dropped to his knees next to the woman he loved.

John's clothes were bloodstained and he couldn't find his phone, unable to dial 911 he saw a taxi driver had pulled over to stare in shock at the atrocity he had just committed. When he tried to stand and move towards the taxi-shirt torn, weapon still in hand-the driver took off running leaving his cab unattended. John managed to drag Stacy into the back seat and still shaking, drove towards Mercy

Hospital.

From the sound of sirens the police were clearly out in force, though just driving down Michigan you couldn't tell that anything was wrong. The streets were almost serene. The few people walking around were oblivious as to what had just happened blocks away, and to the occasional police car flying past. Life in the big city meant nothing could surprise the populace, but give them all a few hours, and their entire worlds would be turned upside down. Inside the cab, Stacy had become deathly pale and was barely making any sound. Her eyes had become dull and unresponsive. It was clear to even the untrained eye, she was losing a lot of blood, too much blood. He begged her to stay with him, but she gave no noticeable response. All he wanted was to hold and comfort her, but there was no way to even hold her hand. He was kept away by the safety glass that was supposed to keep the passenger away from the driver, not the other way around. Stacy was clearly lost in pain and shock. He knew his only chance was to get her help as soon as possible. There was so much blood. When he finally pulled in front of the ER it was full of abandoned vehicles. Screaming for help, he abandoned the borrowed cab at the end of the line and carried Stacy through the front door.

Inside the doors, a clearly stressed nurse asks, "another bite?" without looking up from the patient she was bandaging. As soon as she heard John's guttural scream of anguish, she looked up to see what had shaken him and noticed the condition of his wife. She hurried over to show him how to apply pressure to the wounds.

She quickly said, "We're going to need to bring her into the trauma room now for immediate care." While her head spun looking for help, "Most of those bitten aren't that bad, but she's lost a lot of blood," before running off to grab someone to help.

Within a minute they were rushing the light of his life away to be worked on. The nurse tried to explain to John why he couldn't join his wife and would have to be patient, though he processed almost none of what she said.

After being herded into the waiting room, the nurse promised to return once there was news, then rushed back out to help in the ER. The wounded continued trickling in, each with bites, each one seemed more serious than the last one. Though, most weren't nearly as serious as Stacy had been. The people who were entering the ER ranged from being in shock to near hysteria. Apparently, a group of deranged individuals was going around the city attacking anyone whom they came in contact with and then trying to eat them. What the hell was the world coming to, when such madness was allowed to walk the streets and do this to strangers, to his love?

He couldn't pace and couldn't sit still. Time was against him, while the seconds stretched to eons. All he could do was wait on the news he couldn't expect to be good. All of that blood. She had appeared to lose more than they went through testing in one of the labs each day. All of that blood, trickling into the mouths of those madmen. Now, he had to wait while some second rate, third shift doctor butchered his wife. If he could have only gotten her to one of his offices and gotten his specialists to work on her. Even though they hadn't practiced in years, they were the brightest minds of their generations. The research they were doing would have to be able to help. *Anything but a public hospital,* he thought in an egocentric distrust of anything 'common' from having too much money for too long. He could still hear the sound of chewing in his mind. Looking down, he realized his hands were shaking, and his thoughts were spiraling out of control. He needed to focus.

"Stop it," He choked out. "Just stop it." this time with more force. The pounding in his head started to recede. This is not how he was able to build up an empire, in a field he had no direct knowledge of. He needed to focus. He was better than this.

"Calm down," this time with an authority more fitting to how he always perceived others should view him. Imagine if any of his employees had seen him act like that, or the board of directors, or his cousin. Using willpower alone, he finished calming down and started to put himself into a position where he could be of use. He went through his wife's purse and instead of grabbing her phone found his nestled within. He left a voice mail with his cousin saying he was in the hospital, but once things were under control, and his wife was stable, they needed to meet at the office with their media advisers. Something was happening, and their resources could be used in a way to help. You couldn't buy the type of PR this attack would give them, if they played it right.

While attempting to keep himself distracted from what was going on, he tried to focus on Wotes. The company he helped build, could both help the city and benefit from this situation. If he could just keep trying to think of how he could use his resources to help others, he could hide from the reality of his wife being operated on down the hall. It didn't help that the door was open and he kept hearing snippets of conversations from the nurses' station which was next to the room.

"The bitten patients have sky rocketed"

"Anyone bitten doesn't stop bleeding without medicine or bandages."

"One of the patients read online there were mass biting incidents stretching from all of the states in the Midwest up through New York. It's as if everyone in the east coast has lost their minds!"

If this was an epidemic, a new drug, or a cult, there could clearly be something he could help attempt to put an end to. Right as John was reaching for his phone again, a nurse rushed in.

"Stacy is in recovery room 4. She's lost a lot of blood but appears to be in stable condition. She's been unresponsive and asleep since getting out of surgery, but she should be fine. I can show you to her, but you'll need to let her rest. If she wakes up you can stay with her but let her recover."

As they walked to the room, he had to ask the nurse, "You had mentioned something about with other patients that their bleeding wouldn't stop without medicine or bandages. Do you have any idea what is causing that to happen?"

The nurse just looked at him before responding.

"I've never seen anything like it before. Even minor bites or scratches won't stop without some form of outside interaction. It's almost as if the blood won't clot at all without being kick-started." She paused at a door, "Here's the room Stacy's is in. She's in the far back on the left. I'll be back to check on you soon. I know you want to talk to her, but let her rest. Don't wake her up needlessly," and then rushed off.

John walked slowly past the other three sleeping patients to his wife and brushed the hair off her face, as he lightly kissed her forehead.

"The worst is over now hon'. You'll be able to get better now."

He moved the curtain out to give them privacy, looked at his wife and told her he loves her, before sitting down and diving back into contacting his cousin and staff members. Now that Stacy would be alright, he could try to work. Sitting idly by and waiting just wasn't in his personality.

◊ ◊ ◊ ◊

A loud buzz broke John from his memories, and he was back to staring over the city of Chicago, cigarette in hand once more almost burned to the filter. The TV had gone to the National Emergency Broadcast, and the blare of the warning was turning to a news report. A CDC spokesperson is sitting, sweating, and staring at the report in his hands.

"Ladies and gentlemen, an outbreak has started to spread across our great nation. Currently, we do not have a cure, but it is easily contained, as long as you avoid direct contact with the infected. The disease has been spreading rapidly, due to no one understanding the nature of the infection or how it is transmitted. As you know, people across the nation have been biting others. Anyone who becomes bitten is infected. Some are saying they have seen increased exposure by being in physical contact with the infected as a cause for the spread of the disease." We do not have all of the information on this disease yet. While there is currently no cure, we urge those who are infected to report to both hospitals and police stations for quarantine and restraint to prevent further outbreaks. Plus you will be quickly available to receive the cure once we have it."

At the bottom of the screen a list of emergency numbers and shelters in the area was scrolling. After completing, the message looped. John went to light another smoke as he turned off the TV, letting his apartment fall back into silence. As he walked out on the balcony, he finally had a plan that would solve everything.

◊ ◊ ◊ ◊

The waiting room hadn't been so silent. Sitting by his wife, he had long given up trying to call anyone and was shooting off a barrage of text messages and e-mails. Clearly, the phone system was down if he still couldn't get anyone to answer. While there was a growing queue of outgoing messages stacking up, they were occasionally filtering through. He knew that in no time, the knowledge he could provide, of the bites, would be invaluable. Also valuable would be the steady stream of subjects who were already bitten within the hospitals that they could gather up. From their pool of test subjects they could easily have plenty of uninfected to run time trials with for rate of infection... As long as he was able to get things in the works he could get through anything. Now though, all he had left to do was sit and hold his wife's hand. He stared off into nothing, mind a million miles away, still trying to avoid the reality of what had already happened today. Occasionally, he could hear running feet outside of his room, or a scream from down the hall, as someone new was being admitted. For what seemed like an eternity all he could do was sit there and wait.

His phone started to make a sound. Finally, he was getting through to someone. Get his ideas out there. Get working on a plan. Not being stuck waiting. Finally, he could get his business get on top of whatever this was and beat it. All of that flashed through his mind, as he was waking up. He couldn't believe he had passed out at all, let alone for it to feel so late. But it wasn't his phone at all. It took his ears a moment to catch up to his thought process.

There was a sound, but it wasn't his phone. It was the heart monitor of the patient from across the room. He had stumbled out of his bed and must have torn the monitor off while getting up.

"Hey Buddy, the nurses said to stay calm." John said while reaching over to hit the buzzer to call for help.

The man stopped for a moment before going back to stumbling forward. He went to the bed across the room and appeared to be whispering to the other patient. John realized quickly that the sound he was hearing wasn't whispering but of chewing. He looked down at his wife and knew he had to do something. She would never be hurt again, if he could do anything about it. Why wasn't a nurse responding to the damn emergency button?

He quietly put the control down, and looked around the room for anything to fend the clearly infected man off with. There was nothing. How could there be nothing? Just then he realized the man was near the washroom. He only had one shot and had to make it count. He slowly got up and moved to the edge of the curtain. He was almost sick from the horror on the bed before him, because what had once been a man was now just torn flesh from neck to stomach. He stopped himself and got ready for the only way to try to beat the cannibalistic madman in front of him.

John took a deep breath through his mouth, to not smell the blood that was still pouring out of the dead man on the cot. It was all he could do to not gag from just the visual. He tensed his muscles preparing for the worst. Deep breathe, steady, steady, and he threw his phone through the bathroom door which lay behind the madman. The monster looked up from its gruesome meal when the phone hit the floor. Not a new source of food, the creature ignored it and immediately went back to what was left of the body in front of him. While John knew the initial sound would probably not get the result he was looking for, he smiled as the monster started to shamble towards the relaxing sounds of singing from the washroom. All he could think, while rushing to pull the door shut and locking it behind the infected man, was screw everyone who told him ring tones were nothing but annoying.

Breathing deeply, he returned to his wife, only to see that she had woken up and was looking around the room.

"Stacy! Thank God!" he said while his brain tried to catch up to what his eyes were already seeing.

The look in her eyes was blank. Without responding, she twitched once, eyes closed, and twitched again. The beeps of her monitor matched the steady flat line that had been on her neighbors monitor, only minutes before. As he started to yell and press the nurses' button again, her eyes reopened.

"Stacy..." was all he could get out, trying to ask if his wife was okay.

Through the steady alarm of the flat line, she tried to move towards him. He went to hold her but finally realized what had happened, almost too late. She had the same look they had. His wife was infected. *This can't be happening,* flashed through his mind. She lunged towards him.

This ended with her slamming against the floor as the wires connected to her, for monitoring, held her back. He tried to back away, but she relentlessly reached towards him, tearing the cables from her with the fury of her movements. As John turned towards the door, she slammed into him, trying to dig her fingers into him while trying to bite him through his clothes. He used all that was left to push her away from him and finally turned and ran through the door, slamming it behind him. Where the hell was the staff he had paged? He needed to restrain her. If he could only get her to his company's offices they could help her. Save her from what she was turning into.

"I'll be back love." He whispered to her through the

window before running off.

As he went to get help, he realized all he could hear were screams in the distance. He neared the first nurses' station, and it was empty. The halls looked completely abandoned. Even the waiting room was empty when he came upon it. The screaming had died down in the distance. As he was about to look behind the front counter, he heard the same sound that would haunt him from his wife's recovery room. Something was eating. He quickly ran through the front door and back to the taxi he had borrowed earlier. He needed to get home. Get in touch with his office's security to pick up his wife. Without his phone, he was disconnected from the world. On his way back to the condo, he knew he had to make a stop. Adrenaline was pulsing through his system, and he needed to calm down. There was one thing he craved above all others, as he stopped at a gas station to restart a habit he had kicked years before.

John lit another Parliament and slowly took a drag, watching the smoke as he exhaled. The last of the smoke left his mouth; he flicked the cigarette and watched as the embers spread off. It floated to the ground so far below and he realized it was finally snowing.

He looked down at the gash on his arm, from where Stacy's fingernails had torn at him and realized he was having problems thinking clearly. He was having problems focusing on the present. The gash hadn't stopped bleeding since he left the hospital. He had already suspected it, but now he was convinced. Apparently, bites weren't the only way the disease could spread.

It was just what Stacey wanted, *it's going to be a white*

Christmas after all, he was thinking, as he jumped over the railing and into oblivion.

MY PORCELAIN MONSTER
by Eric I. Dean

Every kid is haunted by monsters. Some lie dormant just inches beneath the floor, under the bed. They rise through the carpet like a corpse from the earth, only at night, after the lights go out. They wait anxiously–emaciated muscles as tense as cables–waiting for a juicy little foot to swing carelessly over the edge of the bed. Some live in the closet, coiled up behind a pile of old sweaters. They watch silently through that space under the closet door, praying you'll accidentally leave it open (*just a crack*) so they can peer out with curled lips and one wide, bloodshot eye and claw restlessly at themselves while they watch you sleep. Still others would rather catch you at your most vulnerable. They stalk you even in the light, just over your shoulder at the blurry edge of your peripheral vision–streaks of shadow and subtle movements that you try to convince yourself you didn't see. They lie patiently in wait in the back seat of your car when you drive alone, waiting with rigid anticipation to spring up and tear the hair off of your head. They stand just behind you in the shower–haphazardly toothed mouths agape and preparing to shriek…bony fingers ready to grasp your throat as you close your eyes and wash the shampoo from your hair…

…but you open your eyes just in time, and there's nothing there. There never is. You can't see or touch these monsters, and as kids grow up, they leave behind their monsters to torment the next generation of vivid imaginations. Well, I had a different kind of monster, and I couldn't shake him. I saw it every day of my life. I touched it. Cold. Hard. Hungry. Nah, I wasn't molested or beaten. This isn't one of *those* stories. I loved my parents…until he took them away from me.

◊ ◊ ◊ ◊

"Okay honey, it's time to feed the toilet monster!" I was three years old, in the big blue house at North and Bevier—Aurora. To this day, I don't know if I actually remember this, or if I've just pieced it together from Mom's stories—but whatever—if it didn't happen this way, it might as well have. I stood at the open door of the bathroom, mom gently pushing me from behind. The tiles were ice cold on my bare feet, and I wanted to turn around and retreat, but mom's hand was firm against my back. I dropped my pajama pants and walked out of them, glancing back only once. Mom's smile was reassuring. The toilet monster was huge, and his one silver eye, long, squinted, and discerning, stared expectantly from above his broad porcelain lips.

Mom was with me—I felt safe. Confident. I was a "big boy", after all. I stood on the two phone books that she'd placed for me, climbed on, and wiggled until my tiny butt hung into the toilet monster's gaping lower jaw. I had to hold myself up on either side, but I'd done it. "Feed the toilet monster, honey!" she repeated, her hands clasped and her eyes shining with pride. I let loose with conviction, with purpose—sating his alleged hunger.

That was the first and last time I ever used that upstairs bathroom. The very next day… Well, I remember that day vividly in comparison…the paint on my memory's canvas is still wet, saturated in sickly greens and reds that quiver and crack at the edges a little more with each replaying, like some old reel of 8mm film that begs to be tossed in the fireplace.

I awoke early the next morning—the morning that changed me. The air tasted burnt and buzzed with a curious energy even a three year old kid recognized as sinister. I butt-scooted carefully to the edge of my bed and lowered my feet onto the bridge of light streaming in from beneath my bedroom door. Three long steps and I was at the door, turning the flanged glass knob with both hands and hanging from it like a sock monkey until I'd pulled the door ajar. I crept down the hallway with terror in my guts—I still can't tell you why, or what was driving me. Beneath the wandering eyes of an unfamiliar audience of framed strangers, past the baby-gated stairs that lead down to the kitchen, past my parents' bedroom door…slightly open?… quietly, very quietly, I walked to the end of the hall.

I stopped there and stared at the bathroom door, half open and blindingly bright to my sleepy eyes. I squinted against the light and peered, with one eye, through the spaces between my tiny fingers. I leaned into the door, but it wouldn't budge. I pushed again, harder, but something was blocking the door from the other side. I recognized the smell—my dad was using the bathroom.

I shoved the door again, and squeezed my body through the opening and into the bright, cramped bathroom, heavy with sensation. There, on the toilet, sat my father, slumped forward over his knees, the top of his bald head shining, and his left leg leaning against the inside of the door. My dad always used this guest bathroom at my mother's behest—he was a big man, and when he did his business, it was big business.

"Daddy." He was naked. His face was down, and I couldn't see it, but his hands and feet were… purple. Even at three, I knew it was all wrong. The sides of his face were bloated, swollen, and gray, and he didn't look…real. He looked like someone else—someone vaguely like my father, but not human. Black blood dripped from his nose and pooled on the white tile around his feet, running in tiny rivers along the grout. I just stood and stared.

"Daddy…"

The last thing I remember is a scream—my mother's scream—so loud and piercing and haunting that I swear it stopped my heart and froze my blood solid. I remember hands clawing at me from behind, and then…nothing. The film in my head abruptly ends.

Mom said his heart "just stopped working", and as a kid, that frightened me. I didn't realize a heart could just stop. I would lie awake at night for months, consciously feeling my own heartbeat, worried to tears that it might just stop, and then I'd turn purple and die, just like my dad, and mom would scream and lots of people would come to the house and cry. I didn't want that to happen.

From then on, mom would take me into the master bedroom to use her bathroom. I never questioned it. That big white door at the end of the hall stayed shut and not even guests were allowed in it. All guests would use the downstairs half bath, even if they were staying overnight upstairs. She told people the plumbing was broken, and even put a piece of masking tape across the door, from frame to frame, like her own version of emotional crime scene tape. I didn't open the door, and neither did she. We passed it quietly, like a mausoleum, as if my father's corpse were still entombed inside.

One night, two or three years later, I had a nightmare. I dreamed I was that small child again, struggling to push open the big white bathroom door, but at the same time, horrified because I knew what lay on the other side. Still, my body acted without my consent, and shoved itself through the opening, just as it had that day. Inside, my father's bloated, discolored corpse sat lifeless and limp, just as it had on that day. Only, in this dream, my mother never came to rescue me. I was tense, fists clenched and teeth grinding, waiting for that scream…that scream that made my skin crawl and my hair stiffen. It never came. I continued staring at my father, and then his head began to rise. His hands, almost black, wiggled with tremors, and then his fat neck craned and, slowly, his face began to turn toward me.

"Dad?" I whispered, my voice stifled by the thick air, almost like water around me, filling my lungs to near bursting with every breath. His face found mine, purple and misshapen like some absurd clay caricature. His lips hung long and loose from his face and his teeth spread out and waved like wind chimes. His big, pitted nose seemed to bobble and swing like hot wax melting. He opened his eyes and stared at me—cartoonish, glassy eyes, almost too big for his face, and as white and featureless as cue balls. I was frozen in place. My feet refused to respond, and the air was getting heavier around me, squeezing me and threatening to crush me. I struggled to move against it, but I couldn't. I tried to close my eyes, but I couldn't. My father chewed the air and gargled black blood through his piano key teeth, as if trying to speak to me…but before he could, he was suddenly sucked violently backward. His legs folded up around his head and his body contorted and compressed while his arms flopped like dying fish. The toilet was sucking him down the drain.

It chewed and crunched and gulped at him, consuming my dad ass first in a matter of seconds. The last thing to disappear into the bowl was his swollen face, twisted in horror, cue ball eyes staring straight at me. Blood sprayed upward out of the bowl in droplets on the tank, the walls, the white tile floor. Blood frothed out from under and over the seat, and ran down every curve of the porcelain, gathering into a writhing, bubbling, mass around the base of the toilet. The toilet crunched loudly from within, no doubt chewing his bones, and the black mass oozed steadily toward my tiny feet. I screamed silently and my body ached with my need to move...to run...to escape from his bathroom and flee into my mother's arms at the other end of the hall. I couldn't.

The black ooze enveloped my feet—cold, viscous, and stinging with pins and needles as if my feet had fallen asleep at its touch. It grabbed tightly and began to pull. Suddenly, I was sliding across the tile, standing upright, and gliding slowly toward the toilet bowl. The toilet was growing, taller, wider, pressing outward on the walls of the tiny bathroom and expanding in diagonals like a German expressionist film. A deafening ringing stabbed into my ears and I began to feel choked, so tightly that I thought my eyeballs would burst. Every molecule in my body was screaming to get free, and yet, I was helpless. The toilet bowl, now at eye level, began to move, to undulate, and lean toward me as I slid on the soles my feet to meet it, until I could see straight into it. The water didn't pour out—it stayed firmly in the bowl, spinning like a black whirlpool that seemed to stretch infinitely into the void of space. The ringing in my ears became fractured, roughly textured, and wet, like a toilet flushing, but more...organic. The toilet monster had eaten my father, and now it was going to eat me.

Just as my head was being pulled into the darkness, I heard it...from somewhere in the void, beyond the black whirlpool…that scream. That ice cold, splintered-bone, curdled-blood shriek that tore through my mother's throat so many years ago. It came from all around me…from inside the toilet monster. It was coming from me.

◊ ◊ ◊ ◊

I awoke screaming at the top of my lungs, drenched in sweat, in a hot puddle of my own urine and feces, my mother tearing into my room in a flowing white nightgown like a pale, gaunt specter in full flight.

We moved out of the house the next week and stayed with my mother's parents across town in Boulder Hill until we eventually got our own small place just down the street from them. I never had the dream again, nor did I see the house again for many years. As I grew, I would find out that my father had actually died of a massive heart attack due to his weight and bad health, and his body had been there for many hours before I'd found him. He was 38. I would also learn that my grandparents had taken over the mortgage payments in the hopes that someone in the family would want the house again—the big house my grandparents had raised my mother in before giving it to my parents as a wedding present only two years before I was born. No one ever did.

I'd been a late baby for my parents, who didn't marry until they were both in their 30s—a first marriage for both—and I, the only child, a miracle for my mother who'd been told she wasn't able to conceive. My grandparents were also older and eventually could no longer afford the payments on two houses, nor were they physically able to live in a two story house. When I was 15, my mother decided to rent out the big house at North and Bevier to offset the cost. She would go there for two or three hours every day for a week after she left work in downtown Aurora, just to clean and repaint. I wanted to help but…I always found a reason not to: baseball practice, homework, helping the grandparents, or just "not feeling up to it." Still, I would always promise to come and help soon. On the fifth day of cleaning, a Friday, I got off the bus at home and found my dinner waiting in the oven. Mom had left a note. "Cleaning the old house. Turn the oven off. I'll be home at 8. I love you, Mom."

The guilt of not helping my mother was crippling. I knew it was wrong, but I was still afraid of that place. I knew it was ridiculous. I knew monsters weren't real, and I knew my dad's death was a consequence of his own bad choices, and nothing more. I knew these things, and yet…I couldn't stomach the thought of going back there. In an effort to ease the weight of the guilt, I cleaned our own small house that evening. I scrubbed our one, happy little toilet, and I washed every window. I did the laundry, the dishes, and even swept the driveway…which is when I noticed the sunset. How long had it been? 8:30. She was a half hour late. That wasn't like her. It was before the age of cell phones, and I wasn't yet old enough to drive, so I had only two options: either call the old house, or just wait patiently. Mom hadn't set up phone service at the old house again yet, so…I waited. At 9:00, I phoned my grandparents down the street.

"Hello?"

"Grandma, it's me. Mom isn't home from the old house yet. She left a note saying she'd be here an hour ago."

"I'm sure she's fine, honey. She probably stopped to get groceries or just lost track of time over there. Don't worry."

"Alright. I love you."

"Love you too, honey."

9:30 came and went. 10:00 came. My guts twisted.

"Hello?"

"Grandpa, it's me…"

"It's late. Your grandma and I were in bed, is everything okay?"

"Mom's still not home."

"I see. I'll come pick you up in just a minute. Let's head over and see what's keeping her."

"…thank you Grandpa."

Grandpa pulled up five minutes later in his big blue Oldsmobile, dressed in a burgundy bathrobe with pajama pants underneath. "Get in, little man." He said with a smile, but I could see the worry behind it. I was still dressed in my clothes from school. I hadn't even taken my sneakers off.

We took Broadway along the Fox River to the old house—we spent the ten minutes in silence. The tension was palpable, but every couple of minutes, Grandpa would glance at me and smile reassuringly. I was glad to have him there. I trusted his strength. The old streets were so familiar, though I hadn't seen it in so many years. We approached the big blue house along North, and as we rounded the corner onto Bevier, Mom's sedan was parked in the driveway. "There! See?" Grandpa said through a smile. We pulled in behind her and got out. The house was smaller than I remembered, and it seemed dry and tired, slouching and sagging under the weight of its emptiness. Grandpa walked straight to the door and let himself inside, leaving his driver's side car door open. I hurried to catch up. Once inside, I was stopped in mid step by a flood of memories. The house was empty, but the ghosts of old furniture faded in and out of existence in my mind's eye. I hadn't thought about this place in years, and hadn't been here since I was tiny, but I knew exactly where things had been. I knew the colors of the curtains and the way the magazines would stack on the oak coffee table. I knew where the Christmas tree stood and where my parents would sit to watch television. My grandpa emerged from the kitchen with a slightly worried look, then he suddenly smiled at me. "The place looks clean! Your mom is doing a great job!"

He continued toward the stairs, but stopped at the bottom and called my mom's name up the narrow stairwell. No answer. He called again, louder, with the slightest edge of panic in his voice. No answer. Something grabbed me by the heart and pulled me forward. I ran toward the stairs, slipped past my grandpa and took the stairs two at a time. He called after me, but I didn't stop. I just ran. There, at the top of the stairs, I saw the light streaming from the open door of the guest bathroom, cutting a diagonal line across the dark brown shag carpet that crooked and crept up the far wall. I topped the stairs and rounded the corner to the left, and time slowed.

I moved as if in a dream. Effortlessly. Gracefully. I hovered inches above the floor and glided into the bathroom holding half a breath. There on the white tile, in a puddle of fresh, crimson blood, lay my mother. Her eyes were half open, but rolled up, and her body was contorted as she lay on her back on the small floor, yellow rubber gloves on her hands and bottles of cleaning chemicals strewn about. I fell to her side and grabbed her face. I must have been screaming, but I heard nothing. Hands. They grabbed at me from behind again. They pulled me, but I refused to let go. Strong, thick hands lifted me away from my mother and back out into the darkness of the hallway. I turned to see my grandfather, red faced and gasping for breath. His lips formed words, but I couldn't hear them. He stood taller than I've seen him in years, and his eyes weren't panicked at all. He looked strong and full of authority. He looked at my mother for only a second before pushing me gently to one side and easing himself painfully down to her side. He clutched her face and neck in his hands. He turned to me. More words. He turned back to her and slapped her face gently, his lips moving. He turned to me again. More words. Firm, hard words. I still couldn't hear them. He repeated them, and as if echoing from faraway walls, I heard the softest reverberation of "Get Help!" I stood for only a second. I saw my mother's eyelids flutter, and her eyes rolled forward and looked at my grandfather, and then at me, and I ran.

I ran downstairs and out the front door. I ran into the dark, silent street, and I froze. Where do I get help? Who is here to help me? In the midst of the moment, an image rose up from the dark basement of my brain—an image of a giant, living toilet with a black whirlpool in its throat. The sound of a scream from beyond the void grew louder and louder. White light grew in intensity around me until I felt like I was going to pass out. I turned to the left. Headlights. The scream became a car horn.

There I was, standing in the middle of Bevier while a truck sat only a few feet away, headlights flashing, horn blaring. I couldn't see into the windshield, and I did the one thing I knew to do.

"HELP!" I don't know if I screamed it once, or a thousand times, but in seconds, a man had emerged from the truck and grabbed me by the shoulders, demanding to know what was wrong. I pointed to the open door of the old house. "MY MOM! SHE NEEDS HELP!"

The man ran toward the old house. Neighbors had appeared from their houses to investigate the commotion. One of them took me into the front yard of the old house and hugged me. The man ran back out from my house and spoke with some of the neighbors. They hurried into their respective houses. Still others gathered in groups and talked quietly, staring at me with confusion and worry. Distant sirens grew louder. Lights. Police. Paramedics. My mother on a stretcher. "She'll be okay," one of them said, "she's alive. She'll be okay." My grandfather guided me to his car and buckled me in.

My grandparents and I sat silently in the waiting room of Aurora Medical Center until dawn. One doctor emerged and told us she was talking, but with difficulty. They said she remembered cleaning and getting light headed. The police said she'd likely passed out from the fumes and fallen backward, splitting the back of her head open on the edge of the toilet bowl. Later, a doctor would approach cautiously and tell us that her brain was swelling and that she needed surgery immediately. Still later, they'd say that parts of her brain had been severely affected by the trauma, and that her vitals weren't stabilizing. At some point around dawn, they told us she'd passed.

The rest of that year is pretty much a blur. There was a lot of crying and hugging. There was a funeral. More crying and hugging. I moved in with my grandparents in Boulder Hill, and it was awhile before I went back to school, but I did go back. To be honest, I can't really remember much of it. I slept a lot. I guess I did most of the things a normal kid does. I wasn't irreparably damaged by the loss of my parents. If anything, I felt numb. I didn't have any more nightmares after that. Hell, I didn't really dream at all anymore. I lived, I worked, I played, I loved, and I lost. Life goes on. My grandparents sold both my mother's house in Boulder Hill and our old blue house at North and Bevier and used the money to send me to Bradley University in Peoria—my grandpa's alma mater. I graduated with decent grades and a business degree and moved to Chicago. I've been married and divorced since then, though I've never had a kid of my own. I wasn't verse to it…it just never felt right. I visited my grandparents on the holidays until they died, two years apart, of various natural causes. They died comfortably and happily: my grandfather asleep in his own bed, and my grandmother in a hospital, surrounded by family. They died respectfully – with dignity.

◊ ◊ ◊ ◊

After my grandparents died, I didn't have much reason to go back to Aurora. So, I've never been back. It's been about five years now, I think. I never would've gone back, either… hell, I wouldn't have done a lot of things if not for that goddamn news article.

◊ ◊ ◊ ◊

"Hey, didn't you grow up there? Did you know that guy?" My coworker slid the newspaper in front of me and pressed a greasy finger just below the headline, "FATHER OF FOUR COMMITS SUICIDE". I read the name.

"No, I didn't know him." I started to slide the paper away from my ham and cheese sandwich, until my eye caught the fuzzy, black and white photo near the bottom of the article. An ambulance was parked outside of an old, two-story house that seemed to sag beneath its own weight. I slid the paper back toward me and started to read the article. Police say his body was discovered in an upstairs bathroom. I slid the paper away.

That night, I dreamed. It was the first dream I can remember in fifteen years. A long hallway with brown shag carpet. *God, no.* A big white door—so much taller than me, and widening at the top, and leaning out over me like a surreal authoritarian. Blinding white light streaming from a widening crack. *Please, not this.* I am being pulled toward the light. My tiny feet aren't even touching the ground. My stiff body is being held aloft and moved slowly forward, through the door. I struggle, but I am weak. I can't move. *Someone, please wake me up...* I move into the bathroom. My ears are ringing painfully. My skin tingles, and my face begins to burn with a feverish heat. My eyes adjust to the room. The angles are wrong. There are no parallel lines here. The walls, ceiling, and floor are warped and stretched, breathing and pulsing with every heavy beat of my heart. The tile floor is a discordant mosaic of sterile white, misshapen tiles. In a distant corner sits the toilet. It twists on its bolts to face me. The floor between us begins to shorten, though neither of us are moving. *God, please don't make me see this again!* A sudden squeaking, a jarring screech of rubber across wet tile. I turn my head to see my mother—her body is long and slack, as if her joints aren't fastened correctly. She slides across the long, tile floor as if pulled violently by an unseen hand. It slings her side to side in a serpentine trail across the impossibly long floor, leaving a wide, cherry red trail of streaking blood behind her. Her bright yellow rubber gloves clutch wildly at the tile, but find no purchase. Her legs wobble and flop like snakes as her body slides like a strawberry blonde mop. Her skin is as white as the tile. Her eyes...open, but empty, lifeless, and brilliantly white. She suddenly stops at my feet and falls limp. The bathroom has become small around us, crushing us. The toilet is there, right in front of us—larger than life and vibrating with an electric intensity that prevents me from looking directly at it without feeling nauseous. I see the lid, in my periphery, slam open, as the toilet begins to warp, and lean over toward us. The bowl grows wide. That familiar black hole of swirling darkness.

My mother's body begins to slide in. Squeaking rubber and streaking blood across white tile. Her arm suddenly shoots out straight and her yellow gloved hand grabs my ankle like a vice. Her pale face lifts up to me, twisted in disgust—her white eyes burning. She speaks without moving her lips, and the whispered words echo inside my skull.

"Why didn't you come help me?"

I awake screaming in wet, warm sheets.

◊ ◊ ◊ ◊

I pull up slow and park my car alongside the curb on Bevier. Pulling into the driveway doesn't feel right. This isn't my house. I mean, technically it was…is. It took me all of six months to get the house again. After what happened, the family was eager to sell. They took my first offer. I closed this morning. I rub the key between my thumb and forefinger and glance up the house, and I just as quickly look away. This isn't my home anymore.

I hadn't bothered to get the utilities turned on. I wouldn't be staying that long. I step out onto the street. The pale green street light hums and tiny bits of gravel crunch between my feet and the cracked concrete. I pop the trunk. The warm yellow light is comforting, and for an instant, I consider crawling in, closing the lid, and hiding until morning. I take a deep breath. I need this.

I put the key between my lips—its bitterness seems fitting. I pick up the battery powered lantern in my left hand, the tag still hanging from the handle, and I pick up the duffle bag in my right. I'm trying not to think too far ahead about what I'm doing here. I keep my plans short…simple. One foot in front of the other. Face the door and walk. Step up on the curb. Deep breath. I put the bag down long enough to unlock the door. My right arm is shaking. Another deep breath. Put the key in slowly, turn. The lock sticks. I turn it harder. Click.

The door swings open on an empty house. The creak echoes through empty rooms, waking up the spirits of old furniture, familiar paint, the distant sounds of ancient indiscernible voices, like wind through the trees. Up the stairs that seem to last forever. Two. Three. Four. I count the steps to keep my mind blank. Seven. Eight. Nine. Ten. The lantern emits a hot white light that shines through the banister posts. A chorus line of dancing shadows on the far wall to the right. The weight of the duffle bag tugs at my shoulder. I reach the top of the stairs. Deep breath.

I turn slowly to my left. The door. Still white. It seems…so much smaller now. I stare at the knob for a few moments. With one motion, I slide the large handle of the lantern over my hand and onto my wrist, and I open the door with my left hand. Immediately, I let it slide back down into my hand, and I hold it up between me and…and…an empty bathroom. White tile. I step inside. I close the door with my foot, and there it is. A cold shiver dances across my ribs, and my breath falters. The same toilet. It also seems…so goddamn small. The lantern light falls across its curves casting shadows like wrinkles across its aging face.

"I knew you'd come," it seems to say to me. "I haven't forgotten you."

I look up and see the pellet holes and staining in the popcorn ceiling. I set down my lantern and duffle bag, and draw the tab down the long, loud zipper.

"I dreamed about you last night," I say aloud. "I didn't realize how much I'd grown."

I reach inside the duffle and pull out my grandfather's rusted sledge. It was one of the few things I kept from the estate sale. I didn't know why, at the time, but now, standing here, holding it in my sweating hands, twisting my palms against the lacquered wood handle, it all makes sense. For the first time, I stare into his one chrome eye and I take a deep, slow breath. I am not afraid. I tell him so.

"I'm not afraid of you."

He is silent.

I hold the sledge high above my head, and I clench my teeth and growl, bringing it down hard and smashing the toilet tank into two pieces that fall off on either side. I raise it again, this time shattering the plastic toilet seat and knocking a large piece of the bowl off the right side. I raise it again. And again. And again. And again. I smash the toilet down to the bolts. I smash every piece until no bit is larger than my palm. I'm heaving, choking, crying aloud. Tears roll down my face, and spit hangs from my lips in strings. I can't stop. I cry for my father, and I cry for the mother I never mourned. I cry for a terrified child too small to face his fear. I fall to my knees and I weep over the battered, dismembered corpse of my monster, and for the first time in my life, I feel like a man.

I close the door behind me. The air is clean, and I breathe it through the smile of a free man. The pale green streetlight hums, and the night sky greets me like a brother. I walk tall toward the soft yellow light of my open trunk. The world seems a little smaller. I know I'll sleep like a baby tonight.

'

PIASA REMAINS
by Herika R. Raymer

"With a scream of agony, the Piasa Bird released its hold on Ouatoga and plunged down the bluff to disappear forever in the swift waters of the great river." –The Legend of the Piasa Bird

E ric Costello had a bad feeling.

He and his friends were just leaving the site of the Piasa Bird in Alton. It was a two hour drive to Peoria, where they would pitch tents in the Wildlife Prairie State Park for the weekend. It did not hurt that the Old English Fair was also happening that weekend, so there would be tournaments, music, dancing, and other activities. It was supposed to be fun.

So then why did he feel cold? His stomach was heavy and his throat felt tight. He had made this annual jaunt for about several years now, what was different this time?

He looked to his right and then in the rearview mirror, taking in his friends and wondering if they were what was different. Not possible. They had been coming with him for the past few years. It was not as if there was someone new in the mix.

Alice Earle sat behind him, looking at her phone and typing on the keypad—undoubtedly talking to one of her daughters—while her husband, Matt, was talking with Angelia Issac. Angelia had just graduated college and this trip was part of her celebration. Ted Hayden sat in the passenger seat, tapping his knee idly to the rhythm of the radio. Eric had known them all for years. Ted and Angelia he had gone to school with, and Alice and Matt were part of his gaming group. They had been brought together at an accidental meeting at the Tennessee Renaissance Fair outside Arrington. Delighted to have a shared interest, they started taking trips together to see which Fair they liked the best. This year was Peoria. The drive had started as always, meeting at Eric's house, planning out where to stay, deciding what they were going to do, and then getting on the road.

Since they left on Thursday, it was agreed they would stop by the tourist site on Great River Road in Alton early Friday. It would give them plenty of time to get to Peoria. The time at the Piasa site had been fun, but crowded. Eric read about the Piasa while researching possible insignias for his medieval persona's shield and had always wanted to see the site. It did not completely disappoint. The construction tape was a bit of a let-down, but the image of the monster bird itself was impressive. It stood about 50 feet above the water and was incised into the rock of the bluffs, with the carving painted vivid red, black, and green. He knew it was a reproduction of the original, but it was still awe-inspiring. The huge creature glared over the river from its immortal perch, ignoring the chatter of the crowds below. Its majestic form stood erect, almost poised for flight, and Eric could just imagine it beating its huge wings and swooping upward so quickly and with such force that the people were knocked down from the air pressure. The atmosphere around it was a bit oppressive, but Eric contributed that to the cloudy weather and the under-construction appearance of the grounds. The plumage of the stone horror may not shine brilliantly at the moment because the sun was hidden behind the clouds, but its dark scales seemed to drink in the light as its white fangs shone with anticipation of a good meal. The area in front of the image was roped off, but more than one person braved it to get close enough to take pictures—oblivious of the hungry atmosphere of the image. Eric shrugged and shook his head, trying to dislodge the bizarre picture from his head. It stayed with him, however, and as he drove away from the site he began to feel uneasy.

At first it was just a feeling as though he had forgotten something, but a quick check of his pockets showed he had everything. The further they went, the heavier his body became. It felt like when he was getting ready to give his boss bad news. His entire body was just heavy, and his stomach began to clench. What was wrong with him?

Checking over his friends again, he noticed no one else seemed to be uneasy. It must just be him. Though he could not, for the life of him, figure out what was out of place.

"What'd ya think of that bird?" Ted asked, pulling him from his thoughts.

Oddly grateful for the distraction, he answered. "More like a chimera, and it was pretty interesting."

Ted snorted. "Bunch of superstitious malarkey."

Eric gave his friend a sidelong glance. Ted had a tendency to mock anything spiritual. He suspected the other was an atheist, but he had never gotten into that particular discussion. In the context of the games, Ted knew the deities backwards and forwards, but when it came to myths and legends of any religious type he was knowledgeable, but Eric would hazard to say, disrespectful. He valued reason above belief.

"Yesterday's superstition is today's science," he responded, loosely quoting his favorite black and white movie *The Haunting*.

"Aw c'mon man," his friend mocked. "You can't really say you believe that a big bird swooped down on a tribe and ate the people and finally was killed by poison arrows? That sounds like a fantasy story."

Eric shrugged. "If there is one thing I know, life can be stranger than fiction."

"What're you talking about?" Alice asked from the rear seat.

"The Piasa Legend," Eric answered before Ted could.

He could almost hear her smile. "I love old tales like that. So full of imagination! Makes me wonder what really happened, or what they really saw."

"They were probably hopped up on peyote," Ted supplied.

Alice blew him a raspberry as Matt laughed.

"Don't mock what you don't understand," Angelia cautioned in a sharp tone.

Ted rolled his eyes but wisely kept quiet. Angelia was a self-proclaimed witch. From Ted's reaction, Eric guessed that the two had gotten into more than one bad fight over spiritual matters. Though he did not agree with her path, he was grateful her warning quieted the other down. The more they talked about the topic, the worse he was feeling. The sky was clearing up, but there seemed to be a cloud over him. Everything before him seemed shadowed and gloomy.

The conversation in the car turned to more mundane subjects, thankfully. He welcomed the change of topic, trying his best to be as light-hearted as he was pretending to be. Unfortunately the closer they got to Peoria the worse he was feeling. He was not sick, thank heaven, he was just feeling dread.

Alice provided directions via the GPS on her phone, and it was not long before they were pulling into the state park. There were already other people there, putting up the kiosks and setting in place the posts that would outline the tournament ring. Double-checking to see where they could set up their camping gear, Eric eventually found a favorable spot.

Their tents were set up in a circle by sundown, their gear—both garb and mundane—was laid out inside. Having anticipated being hungry but exhausted, they had already stopped in Peoria and picked up some food. There was very little talking as they chewed. The food was tasteless to Eric as he mechanically processed it.

"Check this out," Ted boasted.

Eric felt himself go cold as Ted pulled out a hunk of stone from his jacket pocket. The color on it was a familiar shade of red. He had just seen it. On the bluffs they had left earlier that day.

He stopped chewing as it struck him. It was not getting closer to Peoria that had made him feel uneasy. It had been driving further away from Alton.

There was a moment of silence before a babble of voices erupted.

"Where'd you get that?"

"What have you done!?"

"When did you...?"

Ted just laughed as he held up his prize. "There were so many people getting past the rope to take pictures that the guards were busy. They did not see me get too close, and when they did I was just told to clear off." He tossed it up and caught it. "Just wanted a memento."

"You took a piece from the bluff?" Angelia's voice was almost strangled.

He nodded. "Damn straight!"

"Have you no respect?"

"Of what? Stone?" he made a rude noise. "No."

"That is a painting to honor the defeat of the Piasa Bird!" she hissed.

He rewarded that remark with a derisive look. "C'mon Angelia, even *you* can't believe that drivel."

If looks could kill.

"There's no such thing as a monster bird," he said flatly.

"You are taking it back," her tone brooked no argument.

His look became stubborn. "You have no idea what I went through to get this."

"I don't care."

Now his expression became thunderous. "I won't."

"Yes, you will."

"Who's gonna make me?" he taunted as he stood up, still holding the stone.

She rose with him and met him, standing in his way. "I will if I have to."

"Ooo," he mocked again. "Gonna curse me?"

Angelia looked ready to rip his throat out, spell or no.

Whatever she would have said was cut short by Alice getting up and making a placating motion. He was never sure how she did it, but whenever Alice got involved in a confrontation, she usually had a calming effect—unless she was the one who was mad. From the look on her face, Eric would guess she was not pleased, but she was not as angry as Angelia was.

"Ok guys," she said in a soft voice, "no need to get too nasty."

Ted and Angelia were standing almost nose-to-nose, their angry eyes never leaving one another. Thankfully, their stances eased a bit. The stone was still held between them.

"Ted," Alice began in her motherly voice. "You should not have taken that."

"And why not?" he sneered, never looking away from his immediate opponent.

"First of all, it was probably illegal."

"So I pay a fine, big deal."

"Secondly, it was disrespectful."

"To the spirit of the bluff?" he scoffed.

"Try the people who painted it," she reasoned. "They put a lot of work into that, and you destroyed it."

"It was recently repainted due to weather damage," he growled.

"And how would you feel if someone came to your house and pulled off a piece of your wall after you spend hours painting it?" Matt asked from where he sat.

Ted said nothing to that.

"Third, you're being an asshole," Angelia added.

Ted said something precise about her heritage, to which she responded about which orifice he could stow his opinions. The argument was getting more heated and now Matt had joined his wife in trying to keep tempers from exploding. Eric figured that was a lost cause.

Was it just Eric, or was it getting colder? The sunset's brilliance attracted his attention. The azure cloak of night draped above him, following the lowering sun. Towards the west was a brilliant display of oranges, reds, and yellows. For a moment, just a moment, he thought the fading light of the setting sun caressed the surface of the stolen stone. It made the red look as deep as blood.

The chills were getting worse.

Finally, he stood and joined the fray.

"Ted," he said evenly, every word felt like an effort, "you're taking it back."

Something in his voice must have belied his discomfort, because all four of them stopped bickering and turned toward him. Angelia, Matt, and Alice looked relieved, but then concerned. Ted appeared as though he was ready to argue, but whatever he was going to say stuck in his throat at seeing Eric's expression. He could only guess what he looked like, if it was anything like he felt.

"Not you too. Look, you're my friend and all but..." he started.

Ted's next words were interrupted by a gust of wind. Cold. Biting.

Not typical for June.

The jeer died on the other's lips. Ted paled and began to look uneasy. Good. At least now Eric was not alone in the heavy feeling of dread.

An unmistakable sound of wings broke the silence, causing everyone to blanch and look around nervously. Eric did not, actually afraid of what he would see. Unlike Ted, he had faith. Beyond his faith, he knew there were things which could not be readily explained—superstition as Ted would call them. Most importantly, he knew not to show disrespect for someone else's beliefs—even if he disagreed with them. He might dislike child marriages, praying to ancestral ghosts, or even having rituals for everyday concerns, but he had learned to keep his opinions behind his teeth unless asked. So if the image on the bluffs was done as respect to a battle from the past, however mythical it might seem, he knew not to mess with it. To him it was like desecrating a grave.

An opinion Ted clearly did not share and they were about to be shown the consequences.

Something dove across the air above them, like a luminous cloud rushing by. The tents shook, one of them tipped over. The fire in the pit fluttered and died. In the immediate dark that resulted, they could see what had arrived.

The sight that greeted them left them speechless.

The bird-like creature glowed in the night, though Eric could swear he could see the starry sky through its incorporeal form. Its body was like a horse with huge wings that pounded the air so forcefully a phantom wind was felt by all of them; across its hide the green, red, and black scales glimmered like the rainbow illusion of a snake skin; stubby legs ended in dagger-like talons; but what was probably more frightening was that its face was like a creature out of the Book of Revelations. It was a man's face, with red eyes, a beard like a tiger's, long white fangs which stabbed upward from the protruding lower jaw, and two white deer-like horns angled wickedly from its head. Its unbelievably long spiked tail whipped in the air as ethereal flames leapt from its nostrils. The flames heading towards the group finally broke their paralysis.

He was never sure who screamed, but they all scrambled to the ground as the thing fired its breath. A shriek followed, causing Eric's ears to reverberate. As it took wing, the friends moved about the campsite until they regrouped just outside the fair grounds. They turned to see the huge orb of the thing circling and heading towards them again.

"Inside the fair!" Matt barked.

As one, they turned and ran towards the kiosks which had been set up. Some of the fair people were staying near the grounds in RV's, and he could see some lights were on. Maybe if they headed towards help?

"Get to the cars!" he called out.

Another shriek sounded as the thing swooped overhead again. The only evidence of its passing was the rapid movement of the kiosk flaps. It was like storm winds disturbing the grounds. This particular storm was not one he wanted to endure.

They arrived at the vehicles, banging on doors and asking for help. Someone did answer the door, to look at them oddly.

"You're trespassing!" the man said.

"You have to help us!" Alice panted. "Please!"

The panic in her voice and terror in their faces must have been enough. He let them in.

"Ok kids, settle down," he went on, trying to sound reassuring. "What happened? Were you in an accident?"

The impulse to answer truthfully was strong, but something stopped them. They looked to one another as if trying to find the right words that would not get them kicked out from this sanctuary. Unfortunately, the longer they waited, the more suspicious the man became. His face began to darken.

"Look," he started roughly, "I don't want any trouble. Especially with the cops. I am gonna give you till the count of..."

The vehicle rocked violently as the spectral Piasa flew by. Its ghostly shriek could be heard as it passed. The women shrieked as the men looked around for anything to act as a weapon.

Their host paused, befuddled by his home suddenly shuddering. "What was that?"

"Something chased us from our camp site," Angelia spoke up.

He looked at her oddly. "What chased you?"

Once again silence greeted the question. How does one say they were being pursued by the ghost of a monster bird supposedly defeated at least a century ago without sounding crazy? Eric would bet the guy would turn them out in a heartbeat if they said anything. He would probably think they were high on something. From the way they looked, how they were behaving, and if they told the truth, he could not exactly blame the man. Under normal circumstances he might have thought the same thing.

But these were not normal circumstances.

Their hiding place shook again as it made another pass, the screech sounding more insistent.

"What is that thing?" he asked more forcibly now.

"You wouldn't believe us if we told you," Ted said in a weak voice. "I barely believe it myself..." he finished in a whisper.

"Someone better start talking sense," their host threatened as he pulled out a phone.

Their pleas for him not to use the phone fell on deaf ears. He began to dial, and then looked at the device with irritation.

Suspecting what the problem was, but not wanting to believe it, everyone pulled out their cell phones.

No signal.

No power.

The phones were nothing more than paperweights.

There would be no help coming.

Shouts of confusion could be heard from outside. It seemed that this RV was not the only one being shaken in the thing's wake. What bothered Eric more was what he was hearing.

"Can anyone see anything?" one muffled voice called out.

"Nothing, what's going on?" another answered.

"Looks like a storm brewing," a third supplied.

"With no clouds?" the first pointed out.

"Probably on the way with buckets of rain," the third maintained.

"Better secure the grounds then," the second asserted.

The sound of activity followed, but it was not reassuring. Their host had heard it too, but he was not leaving them. He looked conflicted, as if he wanted to join his friends but he was undoubtedly reluctant to leave strangers in his home alone. That, and whatever was out there was still out there.

Then the RV's ceiling buckled inward as something heavy landed on the roof. More screams and the men grabbed the first thing they could get their hands on. It only took a moment for Eric to find something. Another reason to like medieval fairs, whoever is attending them will undoubtedly have actual weapons. They might be blunt, but at least they would be made of metal. The familiar feeling of having a sword in his hands was only slightly reassuring. The nagging feeling that it would not be effective against the supernatural undermined any security he might feel.

An inhuman scream preceded a tooth numbing metal scraping sound.

"Ted!" Angelia shouted, causing everyone to jump and scream. "Tell it you will take the stone back!"

He looked at her aghast. "You can't think..."

"Are you stupid?" she practically screamed at him. "What did you see out there?"

He remained silent.

"If it's what I saw," Eric added, "then you *know* what's after us."

Ted's mouth worked, his natural inclination to deride the supernatural finally being overcome by the reality of their situation. This was something he was experiencing sober. Something he could not easily explain away. This was not a shared hallucination or the result of mass hypnotism or suggestion, this was truly happening.

"She's right," Alice chimed in, "you have to tell it you are taking the stone back."

"What stone?"

They turned to their reluctant host.

"What're you talking about?"

There was another thud, smaller indentures in the ceiling in the shape of large talons appeared, and the insistent sound of a metal-scraping scratch occurred above them again.

"Ted!" Matt barked.

The boy jumped and looked very much like a naughty child caught doing something wrong.

Eric approached his friend and took him by the arm, shaking him roughly to break his trance.

"It's gotta hear it from you," Eric said tersely. "Say something!"

The other's mouth was still working, but there was no sound coming out. Eric could see the walls of disbelief being blown apart, and Ted was not reacting well. He was in shock. Understandably so, Eric was sure he was going to have some problems of his own later.

If there was a later.

He smacked the back of Ted's head.

"Hey!" his friend yelped.

The thing above them stopped for a moment. Then it started rocking the RV with more violence. Things came loose from the walls and were falling off.

"Ted!" Matt roared, beginning to get angry. His protective instincts for his wife and friends flaring up. The sound of his voice did not to stop the thing. "Say something!"

"Whaddya want me to say?" he shouted back, sounding scared and pathetic.

Once again his voice stopped the thing.

"Tell it!" Angelia hissed. "Tell it you will take the stone back."

"It's not real!" he finally found some strength.

"You wanna make a bet?" Matt snarled, taking the metal maul he had picked up and slapped it against his opposite hand in a threatening motion. "You want me to throw you out there and see just how 'not real' this is?"

Ted paled and backed away. "You wouldn't..." he breathed.

"I won't let you hurt my wife or my friends because of your stupidity," the man assured him roughly, indicating Matt held Ted solely to blame. "Somehow I don't think your disbelief will protect you from that ghost out there. So," Matt paused pointedly as he tapped the maul again, "you better tell it what it wants to hear!" he bellowed as he moved, making sure the women were behind him as another screech sounded from above.

A thud from the side now, and a long buckle appeared in the wall. The tail was making damage now.

"Boy," their host finally chimed in. "I don't know what you pissed off, but if I lose my home you are going to lose a limb."

Ted might not have believed his friends would actually hurt him, but a threat from a stranger was different. Their host had no reason not to hurt him. The promise of bodily harm broke him of his paralysis.

"Hey!" he shouted at the ceiling.

The thing stopped.

"I'll take it back!" he went on, going as far as to raise the stone to the ceiling.

The RV shook a bit as some weight shifted. Eric could mentally see the thing trying to peer through the metal. Or maybe it could already see through the material. It was ethereal after all. Thankfully, its attack on the RV had stopped. Eric was surprised Ted still had a grip on the stone, but when he saw the other's hand he noticed the whiteness of the knuckles and even the small lines of blood. Ted had such a grip on the rock that he probably could not let go of it right now if he wanted to.

"I promise!" he yelled again. "I'll take the stone back!"

There was a calm, not unlike one before a storm. The tension in the air was heavy. The sense of waiting was almost palatable. They looked to Ted, knowing without saying what the thing was waiting for.

"I'm sorry!"

There was a burst of thunder, a clash of lightening, and outside the a downpour of rain could be heard. The release of pressure was almost enough to make Eric's ears pop. He could almost see the shoulders of his friends droop. It was akin to the feeling of relief he got after coming up from the deep end of a pool. The others could feel it too, he was sure.

It was over.

They waited a bit more, just to be sure. The only sound was that of the storm outside. Their host silently provided drinks and a snack, and they dared not ask for anything more. They passed the night without any more incidents.

In the morning, they checked the outside of the RV. One of the kiosks had been uprooted and was leaning against the RV, oddly in the same position as where the tail was supposed to have hit. There were branches atop the vehicle, to help explain the damage there. Despite how it looked, the occupants of the RV knew what had happened the previous night. Still, before Ted could start rationalizing, Eric led the group back to their camp site, helped gather the gear and pack it into the car, and finally practically dragged Ted into the backseat, where he would sit between Matt and Angelia. He was still holding the accursed stone in a death grip.

They never got to see the Old English Fair, but they did make it back to Alton Bluffs. Eric thought that perhaps Ted had learned from the experience, but his face was stony as he disappeared into the under-construction site. Nothing of his thoughts could be read when he returned. The others said nothing either, though Matt was certain to have Ted turn out all his pockets to be sure no more souvenirs were being taken. Afterwards, they merely got back in the car and headed south.

The drive back home to Memphis was blessedly silent.

VISHNU SPRINGS
by DJ Tyrer

"We shouldn't be here." Jessie sounded agitated as she fought with a tree branch that had caught on her backpack. Whether she referred to the legality of what we were doing or the difficulty, I agreed.

"She's right," I said, "The website said this was private property and closed to visitors. We could be prosecuted for trespassing. We could be shot!"

Stewart laughed. "Relax, Elin, it's a wildlife refuge, not some hillbilly's farm. Worst case scenario –"

"– if we ever get there –" Pete muttered.

"– if anyone spots us, we'll be told to leave. No biggie."

I stumbled and Stewart caught me.

"Careful, Elin!"

"Thanks. Do you even know where we're going?" I asked him. I suspected we were going round in circles in the forest.

"GPS," Stewart told me, holding up his phone. "We're nearly there. C'mon, you're the one who said she wanted to see the 'real America' while you're over here from Wales, England."

"Wales isn't..."

He laughed again. "I know. Man, are you easy to fool!"

That wasn't true (I hope!): Stewart was one of those people who could spin the most outrageous lies and have you believing in their veracity. I'd already fallen for his faux-ignorance about geography once before.

"Honestly, I think you'll like this place- full of ghosts and mysteries," he told me.

"I hope so. I feel as if I've walked a hundred miles."

"It's only a couple of miles!"

"She's including every detour and root we had to step over," Jessie said, catching us up.

"Are you sure that thing's working?" Pete asked.

"Yep! Here we are. Welcome to Vishnu Springs, Illinois," Stewart replied.

The woods began to thin out and we could see a large wooden building, which I recognized as the ghost town's hotel from the photo I'd seen online, only more dilapidated.

"You've really been here before?" Jessie asked. The way her nose wrinkled, it was apparent she wasn't too impressed.

"Oh, yeah," said Pete. "We've been out a couple of times before."

"And, did you see any ghosts?" Unlike Jessie, I was intrigued by the story of the place, the history and the myths.

"No. Not much wildlife, either." That made him laugh again. Stewart found a lot of things amusing. "Not much town, for that matter. Just the hotel, and that's nearly roofless."

The place had been abandoned as a town nearly a century before. The last inhabitants of the hotel, the remnants of a 1970s' commune, had left thirty-odd years ago, the building left to decay and go the way of the rest of the town.

I imagined the place would be scary, but the shady valley was peaceful and beautiful, while the hotel had a mournful rather than spooky air. The Lamaine valley ran through here, from what I'd read, and on either side there were rocky bluffs honeycombed with caves which, so the stories said, held lost loot from the days when criminals moved into the declining town.

"Look, roses!" pointed Jessie.

"The houses may be gone," Stewart said, "but you can still make out where they used to be."

He led us along the overgrown remains of roadways to what was dubbed Lake Vishnu – although pond was probably a more accurate description-and showed us the stream which flowed from it into the mouth of a cave.

"The cave is said to be unexplored; nobody knows where the water goes..." Pete informed us.

"Oh! I saw one!" exclaimed Stewart as we walked back up the stream to the pond-lake.

"What?" Jessie had jumped at his voice.

"A goldfish. A big'un! Leftover from when they made this lake."

"So, you've never seen a ghost here?"

"No," Stewart said, shaking his head. "You hear all kinds of cool stories, but I don't think any of them are real."

"Like that one on the website," said Jessie, "about the guy who heard the sound of metal being pounded from the direction of where the forge used to be?" Like all the other buildings, save the hotel, the forge had disappeared long ago.

"Oh, you read that, too?" said Stewart. "Yeah, those sorts of stories."

"I wonder why they called it Vishnu Springs?" she continued. The name had perplexed Jessie ever since

Stewart had told her Vishnu was an Indian god; it had taken some time to get her to understand he meant Indians from India, not Native Americans. Although the name might have made more sense had it been the latter.

"Oh, let's not start that again, Babe." Pete hugged his girlfriend. "Let's just say old Darius Hicks had a romantic turn of phrase."

He'd certainly been an interesting fellow! His father, Ebenezer Hicks, had ended his days in a mental asylum, and after Darius's third wife—also his stepdaughter—had died in childbirth, he ended up committing suicide after his housekeeper had threatened to reveal their affair. And, while all that was happening, he'd been busy promoting the healing properties of the mineral springs here and attempting to build the town up into a viable resort.

"Hey, did you see her?" Jessie suddenly asked.

We had nearly reached the hotel, but she was looking past it into the tangle of overgrown streets and plots.

"Sorry?" Pete said, following the line of her gaze.

"Did you see her?"

"Who?" I just had to ask, even though I half-expected she was playing a prank on me in concert with the boys.

"The woman."

"What woman? What did she look like?"

"She was dressed in black."

No surprise there, then! I'd read online a mysterious woman in black was supposed to haunt the area, wandering the overgrown streets and vanishing if she was approached. Who she was, nobody seemed to know. I was almost certain Stewart had told her to say it, although she seemed convincingly bemused.

"Oh, very funny!" Stewart actually sounded genuinely irked; I had to remind myself how easily he could pull my leg. As confused as Jessie seemed when he snapped at her, I couldn't believe she was telling the truth.

"Pull the other one!" I said.

"Elin? Why are you all looking at me like that?" Jessie asked.

"Are you saying you *really* don't know?" Pete said, incredulous.

"Don't know what, Pete?"

"What he means," I told her, "is that we read about this woman-in-black on the website. Are you telling us you didn't read about her, too?"

If her continued denials were lies then I could easily see her winning an Oscar one day.

Maybe she saw something, maybe not; maybe it was only her imagination. Whatever the case, none of us had seen anything and the mysterious woman, if she'd ever been there, was long gone.

"Shall we head inside?" Stewart nodded towards the hotel, clearly tired of the discussion.

I must admit that, as much as I doubted Jessie, I was feeling rather spooked and not too keen on going inside. But, I could hardly say so, didn't want to appear to be a wuss, especially if they *were* pranking me. Besides, I had been intrigued at the thought of seeing it and it seemed a waste not to after our trek through the woods to get here. Whereas it had seemed mournful before, the hotel did seem spooky now. Perhaps it was because the sun had moved a little further west, a little lower in the sky, and the barely perceptible change in light levels had made the place seem drearier.

"You okay?" Stewart looked concerned. I must have seemed worried.

"Yeah. Sure, let's go inside..."

Much as its photo had appeared online, I could see that the lowest level of the building was constructed of stone. The upper levels were built of wood and I could see the familiar triangle of the roof end. Did I see movement behind the broken glass of an upstairs window? No, I couldn't have; looking again, I realized it was boarded up. Strange, the way in which the mind plays tricks.

Apparently, the place had been built back in 1889. Given that it had been abandoned for three decades, and been in varying states of occupation and disrepair over the thirty before that, it was in pretty good nick, especially since vandals as well as the elements had taken their toll. They really did know how to build back then!

The most distinctive things about the hotel were the scrawled memorials left by visitors. It was something of a tradition, if latterly an excuse for vandalism, for people to leave their mark on the hotel, from names whittled in the wooden walls to spray-painted tags, a more permanent alternative to the hotel guestbook. Seeing the graffiti, I felt a twinge of guilt for trespassing, being but a step up from a vandal, as far as the University authorities who ran the refuge were concerned.

"See, told you we'd been here before." Pete had pinpointed where he and Stewart had gouged their names in the wood.

"And, just who are Jolene and Liz?" Jessie asked.

"Oh, a couple of girls we knew back then," he replied, casually.

"So, we're not your firsts?" I asked.

"Sorry to disappoint you, Elin." Stewart was grinning. "Shall we add your names?"

"I don't know. It doesn't feel right."

"Yeah, she's right," Jessie said, her voice nervous. "We're already trespassing. Why leave them our names?"

"Fine, whatever." Pete sighed and wandered over to examine some of the more recent tags.

"So, we gonna look around?" Stewart asked.

I was just about to answer him when we heard it—the sound of fairground music drifting in from somewhere, faint with distance. I think we all shivered, even Jessie. Stewart had recounted the story of how, back in 1903, the carousel operator had been killed after his shirt became caught in the gears of the ride. Crushed and torn by the machinery. The carousel, like everything save the hotel, was long gone and there was nothing in the area to make the noise we all heard.

"It has to be a hoax." I fervently wanted to believe it was, yet couldn't quite convince myself.

Distant voices and laughter echoed through to us, seemingly from outside.

Stewart quickly crossed back to the front door and flung it open. The sounds ceased. A moment later, there was the chirrup of some bird and it was as if nothing odd had just happened.

"Has to be a hoax," I repeated, my words almost a manta.

Stewart shut the door, but the silence remained.

"I think we ought to leave." said Jessie.

I was inclined to agree with her, even if the boys weren't. "Me, too."

"Oh, come on. You said it yourself, it has to be a hoax, somebody's idea of a joke. Or, if it really *is* ghosts, what's the problem? They can't hurt you, and a little music is hardly that terrifying!"

"Stewart..." I'm not sure what I was going to say, but just then there was a sound from upstairs like a door slamming. A moment later, creaks like footsteps. Then, the silence again.

We exchanged glances.

"It's an old place," Stewart said after a moment.

Then as if to refute his lack of belief, we all jumped in fright as a piercing shriek echoed down from above, followed by agonized moans, before silence returned yet again. Could it be coincidence? A hoax perhaps, but not a random series of scary sounds, I was certain. 1903 had been not only the year of the carousel accident, but the year in which Maud Hicks had died in childbirth, along with her baby. It was as if the tragedies of that terrible year had been imprinted upon the hotel in Vishnu Springs forever. And, who knew what had followed in the unrecorded years since? There were rumors, but what tales might people not have told? Not everyone who came here was willing to discuss the place.

"I want to leave right now!"

"I agree with Jessie!"

"I think the girls are right," said Pete, his face suddenly pale.

Stewart didn't argue. The hideous mix of pain and loss in the sounds we'd just heard was far too horrible to contemplate hearing again. As one, we headed for the door.

The shriek of agony came again and Jessie's scream mingled with it. Stewart threw the door open. Again, there was nothing further, just silence. Then, we heard the sound of a bird. That was the strangest thing—such a horrendous sound as we had heard would surely have startled the birdlife. Did that mean the sounds only existed within the confines of the hotel? Was it only within our minds, some strange replaying of past events straight into our brains?

We didn't waste time pondering such questions, but stepped outside as quickly as we could, desperate to be out of there.

"Right, I'm going," said Jessie.

Pete glanced up at the sky. "Yeah, it's beginning to get late. We ought to think about heading back."

I suspect it was more of an excuse to cover his nerves, even if what he said was true. I was just glad he agreed.

"It's a shame, I wanted to look in the caves for some of that loot." Stewart tried to inject his voice with levity, but I could hear his nerves.

I couldn't help but laugh, as much nerves as anything.

"Elin!" He seemed offended.

"Sorry," I sneered, "are you a spelunker? Did you even bring anything for exploring caves?"

"Well..."

"Honestly!" I threw my hands up with a snort. "You'd..."

"There she is again!" Jessie interrupted.

"What?"

"I said, there she is again, that woman dressed in black."

I followed the direction her finger pointed and saw that she was right; there was a woman in a long black gown and bonnet standing some distance away, half-concealed by the branches of a shrub. She definitely looked as if she were wearing an outfit from a century or more ago. As we looked at her, she turned and seemed to drift away amongst the trees and wild growth.

"Follow her!" Stewart insisted.

"No way!" squealed Jessie.

"She'll know what's going on!" I think he was trying to convince himself that we were the victims of a hoax, after all.

"No..." I said, hoping he would listen but not knowing what to say.

"She isn't a ghost," stated Stewart.

"Well, I'm not hanging around to find out," Jessie told us, firmly, turning and flouncing off.

"You'll get lost!" I called after her.

"As long as I'm not lost here, I don't care!"

Had she been thinking more clearly, she might have considered she could wind up lost within the former township.

"Stewart!"

He turned and looked at me. He was on his way after the mysterious woman.

"You can't let her get lost."

"Whatever!" He tossed his phone to Pete. "Use the app to get back to the car."

"Thanks, Bro!"

Jessie and Pete headed off into the woods. I stood uncertain, watching them leave and Stewart heading off in search of the woman. I didn't feel like lingering in Vishnu Springs, but was unwilling to let Stewart go off alone.

I shouldn't have lingered. I resolved to go with Stewart, but when I turned back he was gone, had disappeared amongst the dense growth. I almost changed my mind, but knew I couldn't just abandon him. For some reason, I didn't know why, I was certain something bad was going to happen to him unless I caught up with him, and I couldn't help but feel responsible as he'd only suggested coming here after what I'd said about wanting to see more of the country than the towns.

I pushed through a tangle of briars which scratched and clawed at me. Calling his name, I heard no reply. I had no idea where he might have gone.

There was a swirl of black through the trees. Was it the woman? I was in two minds whether or not to investigate. Would she lead me to Stewart? Did I want to risk confronting her?

I followed her. It wasn't as if I had a good chance of finding my way back to the car alone. I followed every flash of black I spotted. There was still no hint of what had happened to Stewart and I was feeling scared.

Then, I had a horrible shock. There in a clearing before me was a carousel. A carousel! There was no reason for one to be there—and the only carousel I knew of in Vishnu Springs had long since ceased to exist following the tragic accident. Putting one here seemed too elaborate for a hoax, but the alternative was just too bizarre to believe. I didn't want to imagine what it was doing here. At least it wasn't moving and was silent; I was scared it might begin to move.

There was still no sign of Stewart. Oddly, I felt some relief he wasn't upon it.

Fearfully, I retreated from the silent carousel until it vanished from sight. I realized I had stumbled back to the stream that flowed away from Lake Vishnu. I hadn't thought I was on that side of the hotel. I had to be more lost than I'd imagined. I followed the stream to where it flowed into the cave mouth, uncertain as to why I did so.

"Stewart!" I'd just spotted him. He was standing at the entrance to the cave, just inside amongst the shadows, and I thought I saw a dark figure moving into the cave depths. Stewart didn't seem to hear me.

"Stewart!" He still didn't respond.

As I watched, he walked into the cave. I wanted to run to him and drag him out again, but dared not move. The cave was evil. I didn't know why, nor how I knew it, but I knew it to be true.

I was alone.

From the woods behind me came the sounds of distant voices and the clatter of hooves and carriage wheels. And, the sound of distant fairground music...

I turned and ran back up the path, desperately trying to recall which way I needed to go to escape through the woods. I found myself back at the hotel. From within came a horrific shriek of pain and I saw the hotel door slowly open as I stood there transfixed. The woman in black was standing there. I couldn't see her face below the bonnet, but felt she was staring at me. She beckoned me to enter.

"Leave me alone!" I didn't want to learn the secret of the hotel. I was certain if I went within I would never leave, just as I somehow knew that Stewart would never emerge again from the cave.

I ran into the trees, desperate to escape and uncaring of whether I reached Jessie and Pete at the car or trudged miles cross-country and found help elsewhere. All I wanted was to leave that abandoned, cursed place behind. I knew Stewart was lost forever and didn't want to join him. I wanted to get home and be safe once again.

I kept running, hoping I would reach safety. As tired as I felt, I kept going, not daring to stop, not daring to turn back and seek another route. To go back was to make myself a victim of Vishnu Springs. The only option was to keep going on.

Wearily, I kept going. Desperate to catch up with Pete and Jessie. Knowing there was nothing anyone could do for Stewart.

Ahead I could see the car. But, there was no sign of the others. Where were they? I ran to it. The doors were unlocked, the key invitingly in the ignition. I yanked the door open, slid inside, turned the key.

Instead of the engine growling to life, I heard the sound of the carousel.

I screamed.

DYING DAYS: GREAT MISTAKES
by Armand Rosamilia

J ack Lowell didn't know whether to laugh or cry when the announcement was made they were shipping out. Right now. Despite the fact they'd only been in boot camp for two weeks, and he'd known from the moment he landed in Great Lakes this was the stupidest thing he'd ever done. He should've just stayed in Chi-Town and taken his beating like a normal guy.

The Navy was no place for Jack. The last things he needed were rules and regulations. He'd already been singled out as a troublemaker.

"This can't be happening. We haven't even been trained. I never even touched a gun," Jack yelled, as his unit ran around the barracks collecting what gear they had. "Where are they sending us?"

Everyone was ignoring him as they got their things packed and in order.

"What the hell are you doing, Lowell?"

Jack turned to see an officer standing behind him, hands behind his back and his face red with anger. Jack shrugged. "I'm not sure what we're doing."

"Are you going to question your command? Your Navy? Your country?"

"Sir, no sir."

"Then get your ass in gear and pack. We're loading buses right now. I want your candy-ass on a different bus than me, because a maggot like you will get us all killed." The officer walked away, shouting at men who were slow.

Jack wanted to give the dick the finger but knew he'd be in big trouble.

"This is exciting, right? I hope we see combat," Scotty Bello said at the bunk next to him. "I hope we kill some commies."

"Or maybe some Japs. Maybe it will be the 1940's again so your stupid comment will make sense," Jack said.

Jack had no use for Scotty, who was so gung ho about wanting to shoot rifles and kill things, and had no personality unless talking about growing up in North Carolina and shooting and killing things. The man was an idiot. And he snored like a grizzly bear.

While Jack was slight and looked much younger than twenty-two, Scotty was only nineteen but looked twenty-five, even when they shaved his giant bushy beard off the first day. Scotty was a big guy, with broad shoulders and strong as fuck despite his size. When they did push-ups or sit-ups, Scotty could bust them out with a smile while Jack strained to do half as many.

Guys were streaming out but Jack had been daydreaming again and half his gear was still on his bunk. He hurried and jammed as much as he could into his duffel bag, knowing when they got to wherever the hell they were going to, he'd be in trouble again.

"Need help?" Scotty asked as Jack began to panic.

"Uh, sure, thanks."

The two got his stuff in order and they were the last in line. Jack was amazed to see what looked like the entire base on the move, buses lined up in front of every barracks.

"What do you think is happening? I bet the camel jockeys bombed us again," Scotty said. "And now we're heading to the airport to kick some commie ass."

Jack shook his head. "Stop talking like that. You sound stupid."

Scotty turned suddenly. "Did you just call me stupid?"

"Shit no." Jack backed up. He didn't want to piss this guy off. He needed him as an ally, especially since everyone else at NAVSTA Great Lakes thought he was a fuck-up. And Jack supposed he was. "But some of the other guys think when you talk like that you sound funny. I'm your friend and I'm trying to look out for you. Trust me. Stick close to me and we'll get out of this alive."

Scotty smiled. "Alright, but I hope we get to carry a rifle."

I hope we don't get killed, Jack thought. *I am so not supposed to be here.*

Joining the Navy had been the worst mistake of his life, and he'd had some pretty damn bad ones. He knew he had at least two babies but so far had managed to dodge paternity tests and child support. He'd gotten pinched for that home invasion but turned on the other guy quick enough he was given probation, and since he was still seventeen at the time, his record was sealed. He flashed through another dozen stupid moves in his short life and knew beyond a shadow of a doubt he'd make plenty more.

"Come on, we need to get on the bus," Scotty said. "Everyone else is going to get the window seats. I need a window seat. If I sit on the aisle I'll get sick. One time my granny took me to Greensboro on a bus and I threw up for hours. You know why?"

"Because you were sitting on the aisle," Jack said slowly.

Scotty snapped his fingers. "Exactly right. So, I can't sit on the aisle when we get on the bus."

"I'm not getting on the bus," Jack said impulsively. "I have a really bad feeling about this."

"But we have to get on the bus," Scotty said.

"No, you might have to. I am my own person. I dance to the beat of a different drum. I decide where I go. And I'm not going on the bus to go to the airport to get on a plane to fly overseas to some desert to get shot," Jack said. As he was speaking the plan was formulating in his head. The little voice telling him he was making yet another monumentally big mistake was pushed down. Yet again. "Have fun being killed. I'm out of here."

"They'll catch you."

"Nope. By the time they realize I'm missing it will be too late. This isn't an orderly thing, don't you see? Everyone is getting on random buses and leaving as they fill. Something huge has happened. We're at war. I've only gone through thirteen days of boot camp. What the fuck do I know about fighting?"

"I'm getting on the bus," Scotty said but didn't move. "Where are you going to hide until everyone leaves? You can't get past the gate, you know. If they find you sneaking around they'll shoot you."

Jack looked down the street and pointed. "I'm going to the Clocktower Building. Right to the top. When I'm sure everyone has left I'll hop a fence. Easy-peasy."

Scotty squinted his eyes. "Building One will be filled with naval personnel. No way you're getting into that tower."

"Wanna bet me?"

"Sure. Ten bucks says you won't get past the first floor before they toss you out," Scotty said.

"Let's make it interesting. Fifty big ones."

"Fifty thousand dollars?" Scotty asked.

"No, dum… no, fifty dollars." Jack put out his hand. "Shake on it?"

Scotty took Jack's hand in his and shook it. "You got yourself a deal. Wait… how am I going to collect? I'm supposed to be on a bus."

Jack pointed. "You mean those buses all the way down the street?"

While they'd been talking, the buses had filled and taken off. Three barracks down the road men were packing into buses. No one had noticed the two soldiers casually standing on the sidewalk and chatting.

"We really need to go," Scotty said.

Jack threw up his hands. "I'm not stopping you." He bent and lifted his gear. "I'm going to the Clocktower Building to hide until everyone on base is gone. I'll see you around, I guess."

Jack turned and started walking down the block, putting his head down when two Jeeps flew past on the street, filled with men carrying assault rifles. What was going on?

"Wait up," Scotty yelled from behind him. "Don't leave me."

Jack didn't turn back, but he smiled as he walked. He knew the big goober would see the light.

Ross Field, the parade ground in front of the red brick building, was clear of troops. In the two weeks Jack had been here he'd never seen it empty. Units drilled on the blacktop and got screamed at for not being in perfect formation. He'd been yelled at almost immediately for not being able to follow along in rhythm.

"What's your plan?" Scotty asked as he caught up with Jack.

"I'm going to walk in like I own the place. It's the best plan and it never fails," Jack said, knowing what a lie it was. This was, at best, a fifty-fifty shot. He realized if he thought about it, he'd see he had about a ten percent shot. Jack decided to stop thinking about it and just waltz through the front door. "Follow me and don't say a word or make eye contact. And look pissed, like you're in a hurry."

As Jack walked in he saw a station in the office to his left, coffee and donuts. He rushed to it, pouring a cup and taking a bite of a stale glazed chocolate donut.

"Do we have time for this?" Scotty asked.

"Of course. Find some papers."

"Why?"

Jack took another bite and added cream and sugar to his coffee before answering. "Two guys, looking pissed and carrying a cup of coffee and some paperwork, aren't going to get any questions. We're supposed to be here, and the fear when you see someone like that is they'll rope you into whatever shit job they are heading toward. People will steer clear. Trust me."

"OK," Scotty said, looking unconvinced.

"Trust me."

"You keep saying that," Scotty said. He found some blank paper in a desk drawer and handed half to Jack.

"Let's see how high up the tower we can get," Jack said.

They walked out and directly to the elevator bank, Jack pushing the UP button and trying his best to look annoyed.

Two soldiers walked by and Jack put his head down, staring at the blank sheet with an angry expression on his face, holding the coffee in front of him. Like he thought, the two soldiers kept walking.

When the elevator doors opened, Jack stepped back. There were three ranking officers inside and none of them looked like they were going to exit.

Jack hesitated. If he got on they might question him, but if he didn't it would raise suspicion since he obviously waiting for the next elevator up.

"I can't believe this," Scotty said and poked at the blank paper in his hand. "Can you?"

Jack shook his head and kept from smiling as he stepped onto the elevator and folded the papers so the men couldn't see what was not on them.

"Heads will roll," Scotty said quietly. "Especially with everyone evacuating boot camp now. I hope there are enough spots on the buses before the gates are padlocked. This is serious."

Jack glanced at the three officers, who looked visibly upset.

The elevator opened on the third floor and Jack and Scotty stepped out, expecting the officers to follow. Instead, one of them was jabbing at the elevator controls.

"We need to get to the top floor or the roof," Jack said. He punched Scotty lightly on the arm. "Nice work. You should've been an actor."

Scotty smiled.

◊ ◊ ◊ ◊

"I can see Chicago from here," Scotty said.

"No, you can't." Jack leaned over the edge of the balcony and smiled. They were thirty floors up and could see a good amount of the base. This topmost floor was empty office space. The buses were lined up in double file at the gates, a long procession. Jack could only imagine how many soldiers were on the move. He knew this wasn't commonplace and had probably never happened before. Something huge was going on.

"Why are we up here?" Scotty asked.

"We're hiding out until the line of buses is gone. Then we'll walk out and that will be it. Sounds like a solid plan," Jack said.

"No, it doesn't. I don't want to go AWOL. I want to serve my country."

"Then you should've been on one of the buses, right?"

"You tricked me," Scotty said quietly. Jack could see he was getting pissed, and that wasn't good. "I followed you and now I'll be thrown in prison."

"Whatever is going on is bigger than both of us. No one will even know you're gone. Stop sweating the small stuff, dude, and enjoy this beautiful view and amazing weather," Jack said. "And excellent company."

Scotty looked over the side of the building. "Everyone is leaving."

Jack smiled. "Maybe your Emmy Award winning acting worked. You spread panic and cleared the building. It will be easier to get out now. Nice going."

"I'm hungry. We never had breakfast."

Jack stared at the long line of buses on the roads to either side of Ross Field. None had moved an inch as far as he could see, idling and kicking white puffs. "Go down a level and find us something if you want."

"You hungry?"

Jack shrugged. "Not really, but I can eat. Find some candy bars and Cokes if you can. I'm sure an office has some hidden snacks in a drawer."

"You're not coming?"

"Why should I? You can't carry Snickers bars by yourself?"

"I'll be right back," Scotty said.

"Take your time. But hurry up." Jack began counting the buses he could see since there wasn't anything else to do. He had no real plan once he walked out and into freedom. He felt bad for wrangling stupid Scotty into this, because as soon as he got the chance he was going to leave the big man in his dust and get home to Chicago. He just needed to figure out how to get to Chicago without suspicion. He had no funds and only the gear in his pack. He hoped a Good Samaritan would pick him up when he hit the highway and put his thumb out to hitch a ride.

Men from the surrounding buildings were now running out and most had rifles in hand. They were heading down the street toward the buses and the front gate.

"Jack, something is going on," Scotty said from behind him, scaring Jack.

"Shit. Don't sneak up on me, you idiot."

"Two floors down they emptied the gun case," Scotty said.

"Why did you go two floors down?"

"The floor underneath us was empty office space. Two down was a bunch of guys running around with rifles. Someone told me I had to get to the third floor to get my rifle and ammo, since we're under attack."

"Under attack from what?" Jack asked, looking at the buses still sitting. "From where?" He looked at the sky, expecting parachuting enemies to fall any minute.

"We need to leave."

"We need two rifles and a big box of ammo," Jack said. "I'm not getting off this roof until I see what's going on."

Scotty hesitated, staring at Jack. "Are you sure?"

"Yes. We don't know where they're coming from, who they are, what weapons they're using… this is the best tactical spot on the entire base. And we're going to defend it," Jack said. *And keep from getting in actual combat and killed*, he thought. "Grab us each two rifles."

Jack noticed smoke in the distance. Something big was on fire. When he turned his head to the left he saw another fire, this time closer. He could see the flames. Was it coming from inside the base itself?

He went out of the room he was in and across the hall, opening the blinds to stare at the water behind the Clocktower Building. It might be an escape route, although it wasn't close and he'd need to find a boat to get away. Maybe it would be easier to sneak out the back door before anything went down, but Jack was very curious about what was happening. He thought it would be better to have an understanding about who they were facing before running away.

Jack went back to staring across Ross Field until Scotty returned, carrying three rifles and two boxes of ammo. "It's all I could find. But we could go down to a bottom floor and check. Plus, from this height, we won't do much damage. We need to get to, like, the sixth floor. I can hit anything from that height and they won't be able to hit me easily."

"I'm not going any lower," Jack said. "I like this view."

"We won't be able to kill anyone from this floor."

"I don't want to kill anyone. I want to hide and survive. I'm not a soldier," Jack said. "This is all bullshit. I even suck at *Call of Duty*. I don't want to hold a rifle and aim to kill another person."

Jack was about to keep going when he stopped. Had he just heard gunshots?

"It's begun," Scotty said.

Jack was scared of Scotty because his normally goofy and pleasant demeanor dropped and his face was a mask of seriousness. He was suddenly a soldier, scooping up two rifles and a box of ammo. "I'm going to the sixth floor. I'm going to defend my country and this base."

"I'm going to sit right here and wish you'd brought me a Snickers bar."

Scotty dug through his pockets. "I found packs of peanuts."

"I guess it will hold me over," Jack said. "Thanks."

"You're wasting time. You need to come with me to the sixth floor. We're high enough we won't be easy targets but it's a perfect angle as they cross the lawn." Scotty stared at Jack but when it was obvious Jack's silence wasn't going to change, he turned and walked away.

In the few moments the two had talked, Jack was dismayed to see the change in the scenery below: now there was smoke inside the compound and men pouring off the buses. Some were running away from the building but a few were heading in random directions.

Jack looked down at the rifle. He had no clue how to load it. He'd never held an actual weapon in his life, unless you counted the pocketknife he carried in middle school. He'd used it to pick up French fries at McDonalds.

He finally gave up but put the rifle on the windowsill and used the sight to get a better view. He scanned slowly, watching each terrified person as they ran. But what were they running from?

Jack went past someone on the ground before moving back. He gasped.

A soldier was on the ground and two other soldiers were…biting him?

This didn't make any sense.

Gunshots were ringing out all over the base and a group of soldiers below were shooting at anyone that came near them, killing other soldiers. *This is madness*, Jack thought. *This can't be happening. Why are they killing each other?*

Jack heard running on his floor and turned, holding the rifle like he was going to use it.

Scotty stopped short and put his hands up.

Jack relaxed. "What are you doing? You almost got yourself shot."

"Do you see what's happening?"

"Yes." Jack turned back to the window as Scotty joined him. "This is insane. Why are they shooting other soldiers?"

"Some of them look sick. Really, really sick. They are biting people. I saw it with my own eyes," Scotty said quietly.

"I saw it, too. I don't know why, though. I just want to get out of here. We need to sneak out the back door and head for the river," Jack said. He decided he needed Scotty at his side.

"We need to defend the base. We're being attacked by the sick. They want to eat us," Scotty said. He tapped his rifle. "I'm going back to my post. I see what I need to do now. I need to stay and fight."

"This is crazy talk. Come with me," Jack said.

Scotty ran off again.

"Wait…how do you load this fucking thing?"

◊ ◊ ◊ ◊

The shots rang out from below a few minutes later, while Jack was trying unsuccessfully to load the rifle. He'd seen it done a million times in movies and on TV but he was afraid he'd pull back the wrong thing or open the wrong side and it would fall apart or explode. He felt like an idiot and gave up. He could still use it to see.

Scotty was a damn fine shot, hitting one of the biters in the chest, but they didn't stop. His next shot was in the head, which dropped the sick soldier.

Jack looked down at the box of ammo and thought he should bring it to Scotty so he could use it to clear the base and they could walk out, but then he put the rifle back on the sill and looked out. Everyone on the parade grounds was looking bad, with multiple wounds and walking around a bit cockeyed and reaching out for those few still alive.

Below the window the shots didn't stop, but it wasn't making a dent in the chaos below. Jack wanted to yell for Scotty to stop shooting so he could hear if there were other guns being fired or rescue coming, but it was too loud. Too many people still screaming on the parade ground and in the streets.

A bus tried to pull out of line and ran up on the grass, striking a few people before it careened into a light pole and stopped. A soldier tried to run out but he was dragged back into the bus by two others. Even from this distance and with everything going on, Jack could hear the screams.

I need to get this gun loaded, he thought. He needed to protect himself. He was going to escape. He needed to escape.

Jack fumbled with the rifle before figuring out how to open it up. He ripped open the box of ammo and shoved one into the rifle and closed it, not knowing what else he needed to do. He was shaking. A panic attack was coming on. He could feel it.

When he slid back against the wall and put the rifle back in position he couldn't believe his eyes. Some of the other buildings were on fire, most of the buses as well. A man was running across the lawn engulfed in flames and no one was helping him.

Those who were sick far outnumbered the living, and even from this distance Jack could tell the difference without use of the rifle scope. The sick were staggering, knees locked and arms raised. He listened for moaning but it was quiet. Except for the screaming from those being killed.

Most of the shooting had stopped. Jack put his head out the window and looked down, expecting to see Scotty's rifle aiming and shooting, but it wasn't in sight. And no noise.

When he noticed the sick shambling toward the Clocktower Building he looked down. The front doors were clearly open because they were walking right inside.

The building will be full of them soon, Jack thought. *If they aren't already.*

Jack decided it was time to leave. He turned to grab his pack when he saw one of them coming slowly at him from the dark hallway.

Jack aimed and fired, the rifle kicking him back.

He hurried and loaded the rifle again, turning to fire.

Scotty, vainly covering his bleeding gut, fell into the room.

"Shit. Dude. Shit." Jack ran to his friend and turned him over. Scotty was bleeding profusely.

"You shot me," Scotty said, his eyes rolling in his head. "I'm going to die."

"No. You aren't going to die. Don't be stupid. I'll get you help." Jack couldn't stop shaking. "Why didn't you call out?"

"They're in the building," Scotty said quietly. "I need help."

"I'll be back." Jack scooped up Scotty's rifle. "Where's the ammo?"

"It's all gone. I used it. I was coming up to get you and see if you were out."

"Oh." Jack stepped back when the blood began to pool around Scotty. "Where's your pack and other rifle?"

"On the sixth floor. Are you going to get help?"

"Yes. Of course. I'll be back." Jack ran off. When he hit the elevator button nothing happened. He was glad he was in decent shape because he'd have to run down the stairs. It was going to be a long jog.

◊ ◊ ◊ ◊

Jack wasn't in as good shape as he thought, panting and leaning against the wall when he finally got to the sixth floor. He went to the offices he thought Scotty had been shooting from and found his pack and extra rifle.

In the bathroom he found a First Aid kit. He also took four rolls of toilet paper. You never knew what you were going to need.

There was also a glass container filled with peppermint candies on the secretary's desk. He scooped them up and put it in his pack, which felt like a thousand pounds after lugging it from office to office.

Jack glanced out the window and wished he hadn't, because it was even worse outside. Multiple fires and most of the buses destroyed greeted him.

The only good thing was the absence of most of the sick. Bodies were strewn about, most of them missing limbs. The grass and road were covered in blood.

He gathered everything he could carry and went back into the stairwell. He was expecting to hear someone or something moving below, but it was quiet. How long before the sick started going up the stairs?

Jack looked above at the levels above and sighed. It was going to be a long haul back up to Scotty, but he didn't want to chance leaving the gear on another level in case they were overrun and had to make a quick escape. Especially with the condition Scotty was in.

Was Scotty even alive? Jack hated the thought of trudging up all those flights of steps, only to see his friend lifeless. But if he didn't go up he'd signed the death certificate for the man.

He looked back down. The only chance of escape he had was to run down six flights of steps and hope there was a back door leading from the stairs.

Going up to save Scotty would take more time but…he could save Scotty. Why was he even questioning what he needed to do?

Jack took two steps up before stopping.

His mind raced with so many conflicting thoughts he was going to get a headache.

He looked up one last time before turning and heading down the stairwell.

WHAT'S EATING THE MOB
by P. David Puffinburger

"There's a military convoy going around Chicago on North Shore Lake Drive. On one of the trucks there is a silver barrel that is marked "XJI-572" you and your crew will highjack the convoy and take that barrel to the big warehouse. I want the barrel, you can have everything else. Have a couple of your goons kidnap about....twenty people and lock them up in the warehouse, we need them for an experiment. We have to test the stuff before it can be sold. And Michael you don't want to disappoint me or big Al, you know what will happen if you fail" Don Ciorolle said.

Don was one of the head bosses of the Chicago underworld and had been since 1916, he only answered to big Al and no one else. For the past twenty years he had ruled with an iron fist, making him the most powerful and feared boss of them all. He had hundreds of crews working for him, but his favorite crew was the Cabreezo crew run by Michael Cabreezo, who was quickly earning the reputation of being the most capable at getting any job done, plus the old man had a soft spot for him.

Michael walked out of Don's mansion and his driver opened the door to his Hudson sedan.

"When we get to the clubhouse you call up all my

mutts and tell them to get their mangy asses over here now. We have a job to do for the Don."

"Yes sir." his driver Allen Basinger said without question.

The black sedan pulled up in front of the clubhouse's main door and a fat man wearing a brown pin striped suit ran to open Michael's door.

"Hey Boss how'd it go with the Don, we got a good score?"

"Pitsy shut your cake-hole and help Allen get all the boys here now!"

"Sure thing Boss" the fat man said then ran off to get the rest of the crew.

An hour later the whole crew entered the clubhouse by the back door.

"Listen up you mugs, we have a big job for Mr. Ciorolle, so no fuck ups." Michael shouted.

After he gave his crew all the details, they devised a plan. They all waited until the next night when the convoy would be going around Chicago.

Just after dark they loaded up supplies and headed for the ambush site. They sat in the dark and waited until they saw a string of headlights.

"Vicki get your ass out in the road, you know what to do." Michael ordered.

To help in the heist Michael recruited one of his whores to distract and stop the convoy. She was wearing only a bra and a slip that was ripped up to waist letting the soldiers get just a peek of her red bush. Michael thought when this was over, he would treat himself to the pretty red haired whore. He bought her off Fat Tony Carmichael for a truck load of cheap booze and she had been worth every drop.

Vicki ran out into road and started bouncing up and

down waving her arms. The trucks rolled up to her and slowly stopped right in front of her. She ran up the driver of the first truck sobbing and crying.

"Can you please help me, my boyfriend attacked me then left me here, and I'll do anything for a ride—I mean anything." she said with big puppy dog eyes.

"Sure toots we would like to ride you, I mean give you a ride" said a soldier wearing sergeant's rank.

"Sarg we can't do that, you know if the Colonel finds out he'll article 15 both our asses." said a young Corporal.

"Shut up Corporal, what the old man doesn't know won't hurt him, and besides I want a piece of this little red tart."

"There's only one other thing Sarg. I want the truck and you're not invited to come." Vicki said then she pulled a Browning 1911 .45 caliber pistol from behind her back, stashed in her bra strap.

She pointed the gun at the sergeant's head and pulled the trigger. Blood and brains coated the inside of the truck. The corporal was soaking with his sergeant's brains and was in shock. Before he could pull his pistol she pointed hers at him and pulled the trigger. His brains, or what was left of them, went flying out of the passenger window.

By now Michael and his crew were in the middle of killing the rest of the soldiers. Thompson machine guns filled the darkness with bright flashes of light accompanied by sounds of men dying. Within minutes bodies were left lying on the road and the trucks were headed to Michael's large warehouse.

"That was fucking easy Boss." Johnny Two Tone said laughing.

"Yeah let's get these goods to the warehouse, Don wants a silver barrel with XJ or some shit marked on it, the rest of the stuff is ours."

"What do you think the rest of the stuff is?"

"I don't know, but if its army stuff it's gotta be good."

The trucks all pulled into the warehouse, and instantly they started going through crates. A few hours later Pitsy went into the boss' office.

"Goods news Boss the trucks are full of machine guns, grenades, flamethrowers, and what looks like gas mask stuff, like the stuff we wore in the war."

"Hey that's great Pitsy lock all that shit up in the big safe."

"Oh and boss we found that barrel Don wants, its marked just like you said it would be."

"Good, did Marko and the boys round up some hostages for the test?"

"Yeah Boss, we're ready to test that shit."

"We'll wait for Ciorolle, have some of the boys put that gas mask shit on, it's hard to tell what that stuff will do and I don't want none of youse breathing that shit."

"Ok Boss."

"Pitsy, send Vicki in here, I need my spoke greased, if you know what I'm saying."

"Sure thing Boss."

Two hours later, Don Ciorolle's motorcade pulled into the warehouse. The mob boss jumped out of his car; he was as eager as a kid on Christmas morning.

"Michael, do you have everything we need for the test?" he asked.

"Yeah Boss we got the volunteers and the boys made a special room so we can watch."

"That's great Michael, let's get started. If this shit works, we're rich. I have some mutt in Europe who will pay five hundred thousand dollars for this shit." Don said with so much excitement he was about to start jumping up and down.

Entering the specially built room all the men stared into a large sealed glass window as the hostages were marched into the room. Johnny Two Tone and Mike the Hamma wearing gas masks wheeled in the silver barrel. With his Thompson machine gun, Pitsy kept the hostages in line as Johnny opened the spout at the bottom of the barrel. He let a half a gallon of the liquid pour onto the floor then he closed the spout and the three of them ran out of the room, sealing the door. After ten seconds the blue green liquid started to put off a thick vapor. All the hostages began coughing and gagging immediately followed by convulsions and shaking violently. Several of the women fell to the floor having seizures. Soon they all started throwing up blood and stomach acid. The vapor changed back into liquid form pooling in the victims mouths ears and noses. Once their cavities were filled up, blue-green slimy pus dripped out of them.

After three minutes all the hostages started to attack and eat each other, then suddenly, they stopped and stared at the men on the other side of the window.

"Oh this is better than I hoped for, my buyer will be very pleased. Michael, clean up this mess and have the barrel brought to my trucking warehouse so I can send it out. Hot damn boys, we're rich!" Don said as he left.

"Johnny, Pitsy, and you boys go kill those fucks but air out the room first and wear those masks, you seen what that shit does." Michael ordered.

Several hours later the room was aired out when Mooky and Hayzse entered the room with Tommy guns and opened fire on the hostages. Bullets ripped through their bodies blowing out big chunks of flesh. The hostages turned to Mooky and Hayzse and came after them, the bullets doing little to stop them. They jumped on the hoods and began tearing out and eating big chunks of their flesh.

A hostage dressed as a lawyer held Mooky down, biting off his nose. Once it was off he sat on Mooky's chest and teased him with his nose while others were sticking their fingers in the hole causing him to scream until his vocal chords tore.

Michael and Johnny heard the screams from Michael's office and ran to the special room. Johnny sealed the door closed while Michael watched his men get torn apart and eaten. An older hostage in his fifties walked up to the glass, stared at Michael and said. "When we get out of here I'm going to tear off your arms and legs then I'm going to eat your heart while it's still beating. You will die a slow painful death for what you have done to us."

Then all the hostages started beating on the glass. Small cracks started to form from their fists pounding. The glass was two inches thick but was starting to crumble from the beating.

"Woo let's get the fuck out of here boys." Michael ordered.

All the men who were in the room bolted to the door. Before they all could get out, the glass broke and the hostages poured into the room. Despite having missing body parts Mooky and Hayzse got up and started for the broken glass.

Bobby the Blob and Stick were not as lucky as the rest of the men. A secretary dressed in a blue dress grabbed Bobby and bit his throat out then sat down to eat the rest of him. Stick was grabbed by two guys dressed like welders. They tore out his eyes, bit off his nose then pulled his intestines out through his belly button. The two thugs' screams could be heard over a block away.

The rest of the crew tried running across the huge warehouse in a panic, stumbled over each other and knocking into boxes and crates that were piled up everywhere. Before they could get very far the hostages were on them. The toxic liquid made them twice as fast and twice as strong as before, so most of the thugs only made it half way across the warehouse. Only Michael, Johnny, Pitsy, Allen, Phil Young and Freddy the Fingerer made it out. They threw grenades at the infected, slowing them down a little. A few of the hostages got arms and legs blown off but they picked themselves up, or crawled and kept coming.

What was left of the crew jumped in Michael's car and sped away.

"What the fuck just happened?" Michael screamed.

"We just got our asses kicked by a bunch of schmucks, that's what happened!" Freddy squealed.

"Did you see that? They must have been shot hundreds of times and they're still alive. How the fuck are we supposed to kill those bastards?" Johnny asked.

"Grenades slowed them down; maybe with enough bombs we can blow them up." Freddy said.

"Or we could try burning them." Allen said.

"Fuck, fuck, fuck, fuck, the first thing we have to do is go to Don's and tell him what happened, his magic shit doesn't work. Allen, head for Don's and make it quick."

The gangster's sedan pulled up at Don's mansion and was met with several large men who were not happy to see them.

"What the fuck are you doing here asshole? The boss doesn't want you here unless you have the barrel. Where is the barrel, you fucking retard?" said Rocky, Don's head body guard.

"I need to see the boss right now. We have a problem, and if you ever talk to me like that again you'll be eating your own balls, dick face!" Michael said.

Reluctantly, the head body guard led Michael to Don's

private office where he was wearing his satin pajamas and drinking brandy.

"Don, we have a big problem…"

"What, what is it you two-bit hood?"

"The shit, it's no good, the volunteers turned into super human cannibals. They attacked us and killed most of my crew. We tried everything—shooting them, blowing them up, nothing stops them."

"Where is my barrel now?"

"It's back at the warehouse with those hungry fucks."

"Well, you had better go and get it!"

"Aren't you listening? If we go back there they will kill us all."

"Ah ain't that a shame? Guess what pus nuts, if you don't go back you're going to be killed so you decide."

"Boss, the shit ain't any good, your buyer won't want it when he finds out what it does."

"I don't give a fuck you moron. By the time he finds out, he'll be dead, now go get my shit!" Don screams as he points a .38 revolver at Michael.

"I'm going, I'm going."

Michael got back in his car and didn't say a word until they get a few miles down the road.

"We have to get some more guys and go back in there, waste those fucks, and get the barrel back."

All the men in the car gasped at the same time.

"The hell with that, I'm not going back in there." Phil Young said.

Michael pulled out his pistol and shot Phil in the face soaking Johnny in blood.

"Anybody else not going back?" Michael asked.

"No? Good, now stop the car and throw that piece of shit out of here."

The crew drove around all night recruiting every

gunman in town until Michael had a small army. When they got back to the warehouse they could see the infected hostages had gone out, grabbed a couple dozen victims, and were feasting on them.

"Shit Boss, now there are more of them. Do you have a plan to kill them?" Pitsy asked.

"Yeah in some of the crates that were on the trucks, there were flamethrowers. So I'm thinking we fight our way in there, get those flamers, and burn those fucks to death."

"That's a good plan Boss, but half of us will get killed getting to them."

"I know, but you have a better idea?"

Pitsy was not the brightest member of the crew, in fact he was completely stupid and often the butt of jokes he never understood.

The small army snuck into the warehouse and was shocked at what they saw. There was blood and guts all over the floor and walls. The people they didn't infect they ate up until there was nothing left. Most of them had gorged themselves and were now asleep. Only a few were still up feasting on entrails, not paying any attention to anything but their food.

Several of the men snuck to vault where the weapons were stashed, while the rest of them made their way up to a loft which looked down on the warehouse floor. Michael thought if they could get up there, they would be able to pick the hostages off easier. The plan was get all the weapons to the loft then tear the steps down so the hostages couldn't get up there.

After the weapons were brought up, the men quietly tore the steps up. The sound of squeaking nails being pulled out woke up several of the hostages and they ran to where they heard the noise coming from.

"Get the fuck back up here!" Michael shouted.

The men ran up the steps with a few hostages not far behind them. When the men were at a safe distance, Michael threw several grenades down the steps. The explosion finished ripping up the rest of the steps, but unfortunately it brought the rest of the infected to them.

They were safe and the infected couldn't get to them, but they were trapped on the loft. They all armed themselves with rifles, flamethrowers, grenades, and every other weapon they had.

"Let them have it, boys!" Michael ordered.

Gunshots filled the warehouse with explosions, and heat blasts from the flamethrowers. The men quickly discovered shooting out their eyes made them blind and burning off body parts slowed them down. Several of them got completely burned up until there was nothing left but a pile of ashes.

The infected were learning too. There were no steps to climb so they started piling up crates to get to the thugs. The crew were able to stop some of the infected from getting up, but they were running low on bullets, grenades, and fuel for the flamethrowers. Michael ordered the men to break up and run for the large office in the back corner of the loft. Many men were bitten, then left to turn so the infected could replenish their ranks.

Several minutes from being bitten, the men got back up, now part of the infected crew. They all had the same thing on their minds, to get to Michael and eat him alive.

One by one, the mobsters fell to the infected as they fought their way to the corner office until the only ones left were Michael and Johnny Two Tone. They were down to pistols and realized it had been a huge mistake to come back to the warehouse.

"Fuck Don Ciorolle! If I get out of this alive, I'm going to kill that greasy rat fuck son of a bitch myself!" Michael yelled.

After ten minutes of beating on the door and walls they stopped. There were no sounds coming from outside the office, just silence. After a few minutes of silence, a scratching noise started. It sounded like hundreds of fingers scratching on the walls, the sound was maddening. Then the whispers started.

"Michael…. Michael" the infected began a chorus of tortured whispers.

"Michael, I'm going to eat your lungs and share your heart with my new family, then you can join us. It's great Michael, you will love it. We can be the greatest gang of all time. We can take over Chicago, then New York, and every city we want, and no one can stop us. So let me in."

"Fuck you Pitsy!" Michael shouted, then shot through the door several times.

"We're going to get in anyway, I'll make it painless as possible, I promise."

"No! Fuck off you fat prick!"

"I'm sorry you feel that way, now we are going to tear you to pieces."

Then the pounding started again, but this time the door had been weakened by the holes shot in it my Michael, so weakened, it began to give way.

"Boss, the roof hatch! We can get out that way."

"Good thinking, Johnny."

They moved a desk and Michael climbed up on it and started beating on the hatch door. The office door started to crumble and ugly pale faces, with blue- green pus dripping out, peered into the office threatening Michael.

"Go Boss, I'll hold them off."

Michael climbed through the open hatch up onto the roof, then he slammed the hatch door shut, trapping Johnny below.

"You mother fucker, let me up!" Johnny screamed.

"Sorry Johnny but I have to close the hole so they can't get to me."

"You fucking prick, you'll pay for this!"

Johnny walked over to the door, took a deep breath, then threw the door open. Pitsy welcomed him by biting down on his shoulder causing him to scream in agony. Pitsy stood guard over him so the rest of the infected couldn't tear him apart.

The rest of the infected started working getting to Michael. Six of them climbed up on the desk and pushed the hatch door open. They threw it open with ease even with Michael standing on the metal door.

Michael started shooting them in the head as they came through the open hatch... The gun shots knocked them back down the hole, but didn't kill them. They simply picked themselves up and waited their turn to crawl through the hole again. After firing forty-eight rounds into their heads he ran out of ammo. He searched for a way out of this mess. He ran to the edge of the office, looked down and saw over fifty infected urging him to jump down. They had surrounded the office, he couldn't go up or down. More and more infected flooded through the hatch opening, slowly walked towards him.

"Wait, he is ours. We deserve to kill him." said a voice from the back of the crowd.

It was Pitsy helping Johnny through the hole. The crowd separated and let the two towards Michael.

"I told you, you would pay for leaving me. I am going to kill you slowly and painfully, you son of a bitch." Johnny hissed.

Michael threw several punches at both of them, but his punches felt like a child's to them. Pitsy grabbed a hold of him, holding him so Johnny could have his way with him.

First he bit out his left eyeball and ate it, and then he bit off a couple of fingers. Michael's screams were deafening to the point where many of the infected had to cover their ears. While Johnny was working on his fingers, Pitsy was tearing chunks out of Michael's shoulders and back. Tired of eating his fingers, Johnny ripped Michael's pants off exposing his manhood. He stared Michael in his one good eye and yanked on his penis hard, then harder, and harder until it tore loose. Michael screamed so hard he tore the back of his throat. Now his mouth was open, but no sound was coming out, Johnny stuffed the penis in his mouth, making him eat his own genitals. Johnny held his jaw and head and made him chew on it, then he made him swallow the remains. When he was through having his fun he stuck his hand down Michael's throat grabbed his stomach and intestines and yanked them out. Michael slunk to the floor and choked on his own blood….

Minutes later Michael got up as the newest member of the infected.

"What are you going to do now Boss?" Pitsy ask.

"……….I'm going to go see Don. I'm very hungry".

A few hours later several shadowy figures were seen lurking around Don's mansion. They were instantly fired upon, but they didn't drop. Rocky ordered the men to get closer and shoot them in the head. When Don's men were close enough, the intruders jumped them and stripped their skin off eating it like jerky.

Rocky stared in horror then ran into the house closing and locking every door on the way.

"Youse assholes stand here and guard these here doors, and kill anyone who comes in." He ordered.

The guards stared at him, then at each other. Rocky turned and ran upstairs to warn the boss and hide in his private office.

When he was gone the two guards looked around and said "Fuck that. Let's get the hell out of here."

They threw the big wooden doors open and were met by what used to be Freddy the Fingerer. Before they could say anything, Freddy jumped on one and started eating his face. The other guard stared in terror until one of Don's men jumped on him and started tearing his kidneys out through his back.

"Rocky what the fuck is going on out there?!" Don screamed.

"Its madness Boss… I think Michael and his crew are here and they're killing and eating our men."

"What are you fuckin stupid? Why the hell aren't you killing them?"

"We tried Boss. They won't die, it's like he said about the people at his warehouse. They just won't die."

The two men stood behind the locked doors of Don's private office, listening to the screams of their men dying and turning into the infected. After twenty minutes there was a knock at the door.

"Don, let me in, I have some business to discuss."

"Fuck you Michael! You get the hell out of here. I called big Al and he's sending over a bunch of his shooters."

"You mean the ones that are dressed in jump suits… They're with us now and they want in too."

Then there was a loud crash and a fat man wearing a brown pinstripe suit was standing where the door used to be. The two men took aim and starting shooting until their guns were empty, then Michael stepped in front of Pitsy.

"Pitsy, eat Rocky please."

The large man jumped on Rocky throwing him to the floor, ripped off his pants off then tearing Rocky's testicles off, shoved them into his mouth.

"I told you, you would eat your own balls the next time we met. How do they taste?"

The man couldn't answer between gagging and screaming. He choked to death then Pitsy spit the blue-green pus into mouth and he got back up standing behind Michael waiting for his turn to chew on Don.

Out of bullets, out of time, and out of places to run Don could nothing but beg.

"It's not my fault Mikey. Al told me to make you do it. He knew you would get the job done...and he wanted the money from those Irish fucks to fight their bullshit war. He made me pick you, so it's all his fault...you know I love you like a son Mikey."

"Yeah, that's why you made me go back in there. And as for Al, I have plans for him too. You see there's not enough of you to feed all of us so I'm going to see him next."

One single long scream filled the rich Chicago east side, then there was nothing but silence.

SEEK NO LONGER THE BELOVED
by Jay Seate

The dark side has a way of finding us all without our chasing it. Throughout my family's history dating back as far as the Civil War, there have been tales of ghosts. As a child, I recall sitting on the porch of my grandmother's house at night listening to relatives tell frightening things, they swapped stories as if trading baseball cards. The characters in the stories seemed to hover around those telling the tales. Several mature trees stood haphazardly in my grandmother's yard. When the ghost stories began, I could almost see the trees changing shape and moving slightly in the dark, ever closer. And whenever the hair-raising screech of the rusty spring on grandma's screen door opened or closed, I pictured a mausoleum door creaking open, and rotting corpses preparing to walk about, stirring from a long, uneasy sleep.

My parents and I lived on the outskirts of Chicago, so some of them often told tales concerning the War Between the States and about the POW camp at Rock Island. Although no battles took place on Illinois soil, a quarter of a million men, 150 infantry regiments, marched out of the state to fight mostly in the Western Theater. But the story that most captured my youthful attention was of poor Rebecca Mason and her lost love. The woman had been married to my great-great grandfather's brother, Yardley Mason. During the war, the unfortunate man had been beheaded at the hands of southern troops who labeled him as a spy. Yardley and Rebecca had lived in a small town in the southeastern part of the state. Legend had it that Rebecca would stare out one of her windows for days, pining away for her Yardley. She would occasionally whirl about the veranda as if dancing with him. After the news of her husband's demise, she disappeared, a vigil no longer necessary.

Time passes quickly for joy, yet slowly for grief. When a neighbor came to pay her respects, she found Rebecca stretched across her bed as dead as Yardley. Knowing her beloved husband and she were never to be reunited in a loving embrace, she'd committed suicide with the use of poison. It was a generation with a history of misfortune, and although her mortal saga ended sadly, Yardley *had* returned to his home from a faraway battlefield in one manner. His decomposing head rested upon the bed next to Rebecca's corpse, or so the story went.

This tale once heard, had clung to me like something not easily scraped off, so as a grown man, I decided to travel south of I-70 and north of I-64 to the small town where Rebecca had been buried all those years ago. I was fortunate to rent a house for the summer, which would give me time to search out the truth of my favorite family legend—to see if truth was, indeed, as strange as fiction.

I discovered quickly that superstition, repeated from lip to ear, through generations, becomes imbued with the effectiveness of truth. The tale of Rebecca somehow retrieving Yardley's head had been running through the little town of Albion, where the Masons lived for over a hundred years, before I heard it. Old-timers were not shy about repeating the tale, embellishing it with each telling.

Adding fuel to the nature of storytelling, I was able to rent one of the dwellings that rested on the property where Yardley and Rebecca's house once stood. My presence seemed to reenergize the legend. Small towns, I found, had a penchant for whatever melodrama and mystery they can extract from life.

I was advised that the house where I took residence was over a half-century old itself, and there were times when beams and boards would creak and moan without the wind's encouragement. Not a sign of anything sinister; old floors often creaked and heating pipes groaned, but given the little town's penchant for tall tales, it all resulted in more fuel for my active mind.

There were also times when an unknown force within the house seemed to take hold. I have found little in life more frightening than when the beams and boards not only creak, but become at odds with their structural integrity. If this was truly the case, it meant the house itself had a consciousness, but dealing with the dead was enough to take on for the moment.

At night, in the dark, I listened to haunting sounds, not sure whether they were merely the howling of the wind through the tree branches or something more…the moaning of restless souls perhaps, those unfortunates with unfinished business which keep their presence anchored to earth; notions I didn't accept in spite of my early indoctrination. I told myself my observations were nothing more than a nonsensical reaction to stories of Rebecca and Yardley and could result in nothing other than to scare the bejesus out of me. Nevertheless, the cold chills that ran down my spine were not a pleasant sensation.

When it came to the tale of my great-great grandfather's brother and his wife, my mind fell into a morass of apprehension. Things began to happen, things that led me to believe Rebecca's ghost was more than a fanciful Civil War story. Sometimes when we come upon something too frightening to handle, we do our best to pretend our eyes are merely playing tricks. The true fright began with my first sighting of Rebecca.

It was just before twilight near a gate separating the house from where I was staying from the street. The eerie tales left no doubt in my mind of who she was as I observed her from my living room window. She stood still and alone, staring at the house, rigid and motionless, her head titled slightly as if lost in thought. Although she was some distance from me, I could tell she was a relatively young woman, one who had not lived long enough to become old and gray-haired. She wore a dark cloak placed over her shoulders covering all else. And there was something more. A shriek caught halfway up my throat before having a chance to exist. She carried a large tapestry bag, large enough to hold...

It was then a cloak of fear settled over me and I knew any rational view of the world I had slipped a notch. Emptiness without end or no meaning following death now seemed a false hypothesis. How many dead wandered the earth searching for resolution before letting go of the world? A visible spirit hovering in this world, delaying eternal rest, required either my immediate departure, or investigation.

Although remaining would require more fortitude than I'd exhibited up to this point, it was an opportunity to open a door to some understanding of what might lie on the other side of death, a look beyond the veil-I had heard my grandma call it. I took it upon myself to research the true history of the Mason property in the county's Hall of Records.

I found that Yardley Mason had indeed been a Union soldier who was probably executed as a spy by southern troops. An obituary revealed Rebecca had married Yardley only a year before their deaths. His bride was known for her "gift of the spirit," what might be called precognition today. Little more was said or written in existing archives other than the fact that she had indeed committed suicide, convinced her husband would never come home to her. It wasn't much information, but enough to feel some empathy for her, if not pity. I had hoped to find pictures of the star-crossed Mr. and Mrs. Mason, but short of that, there was one helpful item amongst the remnants—a photograph of the original house. Traditional for its time, it was a two-story, white-washed clapboard with a long porch and large windows, and bore no similarity to the house I now occupied.

Unfortunately, the picture was without writing or dates, but a man and a woman stood on the porch in posed *American Gothic* positions, common to that of early photography. The man wore a dark suit, while the woman was clad in a white dress and gloves that came above her elbows—a wedding day photo, perhaps. Could it have been the Masons, a man with a new house and a new bride to live in it? The couple were little more than specs as the photographer's intent was to capture the structure rather than its inhabitants. I asked for a magnifying glass in hopes of identification. It told me only the twosome were in the prime of life and that the woman could very well have been the long departed Rebecca. Curiously, I felt like an intruder into the domestic tranquility of the couple and, as silly as it may seem, my intrusion might even anger Rebecca. I nervously put the picture back where I had found it and tried to shake the feeling. I had stumbled into the Mason's private lives at a time before the Civil War was raging, a time before Yardley left and Rebecca began her sorrowful vigil.

I did more than look through musty small town records. Unable to dispel my curiosity, I sought Rebecca Mason's burial site. The old cemetery rested on the side of a hill too steep to farm. There was a pleasant view of the isolated town of Albion below with its elms and oaks, its houses and streets, and numerous church steeples to help distance the populous from the ultimate reality—a plot in a cemetery. If the Rebs had chosen to try a sortie into Illinois, the hill would have been the high ground from which Union forces could have formed a skirmish line and made their stand.

There were no wrought-iron fences or gates nor signs to sequester the graveyard from the outside world. All that remained among a few empty beer cans, coated candy wrappers, and weeds were a hundred or so old stones to mark locations of final repose. Some of the headstones lay on the ground, victims of time or vandalism. A few names struck a familiar chord as families often stayed in an area for generations, but whoever tended the graves of these souls must have been long dead. Maybe superstition played a role, given Rebecca's notoriety.

Her headstone was simple with no ostentatious words of scripture or poetic sentiment, just her name and dates of birth and death, and one curious engraving. *Seek no longer the beloved*, it read, so forlorn, so sad and final, those words and dates. But I knew there were secrets buried beneath the stone as I looked at the patch of unkempt earth. I couldn't keep from asking myself the obvious question. "Did they bury Yardley's head with Rebecca?"

The day darkened. The long grass stirred. I shivered as the breeze ruffled my hair and whispered against my exposed skin. It grew stronger, flapping the collar of my windbreaker and the legs of my slacks. The trees swayed gracefully like dark ballerinas moving to a rhythm only they could hear. It occurred to me that all of us, the living and the dead, had shared the same wind, trees, and the elements of nature. We came from the same earth and our roots always reached down, the living and the dead, woven together in a great tapestry.

I wondered why Rebecca had returned as I looked at the patch of unkempt earth in front of her stone. Why wasn't she settled in her grave? What had awakened her from eternal slumber? Simply thinking about it sucked the breath from my lungs. I looked down at the village once more. The size had changed little over the many years according to population records. It wasn't hard to envision the day Rebecca was laid to rest just six feet below. I closed my eyes. My mind treacherously focused on her final moments, gasping for the last breaths of life. What were those moments filled with? Terror? Sadness? Anger? They must have been lonely beyond all comprehension. Had she expected to find Yardley on the other side?

The horror of the inside of a coffin was vivid in every detail. I imagined her lying within the oblong box, hands placed together as if in prayer, but her rest being something other than peaceful. The feeling of melancholy dissolved as an uneasy feeling of being watched by eyes piercing through time and space overtook me, eyes commanding me to take action. Had I become an outright lunatic, driven mad by the legend of Rebecca? The townsfolk would love that new touch of drama.

Although God remained an unsubstantiated hypothesis, events had shaken me out of my beliefs. Reality was based on a single dimension. Without question, there was another plane of existence. Was it possible for dead people to control the living? It seemed as if the ground began to stir and tremble as my imagination went into overdrive. I would have sworn it pulsed like the retinue of beating hearts beneath my feet. I couldn't bear to look at Rebecca's grave any longer for fear it was she who watched, the one who wanted...what?

I began to feel the vexation of the dead, the curiosity of their state rather than a resignation. Troubled spirits were not at rest. Things existed that were both dreadful and full of sorrow. Could they sense an interloper? Could they wonder what I was up to? It was all too grim. I had to move before I became rooted to the ground with the weight of fear, before the blades of wild grass were given the opportunity to curl around my ankles. Or worse, drop dead on the very spot where Rebecca's earthy remains laid a mere few feet below. It was all I could do not to run from the cemetery all the way back to the relative safety of the house and lock all the doors like a hunted man attempting to burn this preoccupation from his brain before it exploded. That would not solve the issue that plagued me, however. I vowed to end any further research about this enigmatic couple. I squatted on the land once belonging to two people who had entered into local folklore and that should be that.

Of course, that wasn't the end of the matter. The inscription on Rebecca's tombstone had gotten into my head like a lyric of music that goes around and around until you think you're going to go crazy with it. Many believed ghosts sit on your bed at night and stand behind you in the mirror. My most believable research concerning the supernatural had described them as merely ectoplasm with no knowledge of space or time. It sounded harmless enough, but my ghost didn't feel detached. Further, I read that a spirit could sometimes move from place to place as well as create physical manifestations of its emotions, possibly malevolent ones. Additionally, there were cases where an entity could command a psychic force over people or objects. That seemed to fit not only the legend, but also the apparitions I had experienced.

The next time I saw Rebecca, I retrieved my binoculars for a closer look, but by the time I returned to the window, she was, of course, gone. I could have alerted the authorities, but I knew even they could not help in this instance. I wondered if anyone in the neighboring houses might have seen her, but she would surely have vanished before action could be taken. Was she meant for my eyes only? The moment *that* thought crossed my mind, I felt as if the ectoplasm of a restless spirit seeking stability had passed right through *me*. Was I seeing and feeling things others couldn't? Shrinks locked up people like that.

With each sighting, the figure edged ever closer up the drive that leads to my house. The third time she appeared, I decided to confront the trespasser, but by the time I opened my front door, she had vanished once again. The incidents affected me profoundly, forcing me to think about my own mortality. I had never been concerned about the existence of an afterlife until Rebecca came on the scene. Now, what I seemed to be was…haunted.

It was clear this phantom either belonged among the restless dead, or I was losing my mind, now cluttered with not so dead history. Although my sanity might be in question, I was also angry that a manifestation would play such a coy game with my senses and make me feel the fool. At this point, I made a concerted effort to block out this nimbus of unreality, but then I would see her again. As such occasions can induce a habit to the mind; I finally *expected* to see her.

The sightings were usually as dusk approached, not the time of day I would have preferred to see an apparition nearing the house like some impoverished waif wanting to be taken in. Goosebumps rose on my arms as she came closer, the hood of her cloak now pulled over her head putting her face so entirely in shadow it seemed not there at all, sending new chills to tickle the hair on my neck. I had decided Rebecca must want her property back, or the place where it had stood, her house having been turned to rubble long ago. Could she have hoped to reunite with a relative, no matter how distant? A century and a half was a large chunk of eternity to share with merely a head. Or could it be more sinister than that? Judging by her hooded appearance that simulated The Grim Reaper himself, maybe she wanted someone to replace Yardley, or the part of him she was not able to recapture. Could some malevolent force want to stretch forth its tentacles around me in a supernatural embrace? Could her goal be, God help me, *possession*?

I now considered it no coincidence one hundred and fifty years had passed since the final date on her tombstone, the day Rebecca took her life. In my research, I had discovered myself to be the only single man to rent a house on the Mason's property. All of my suppositions were certainly fuel to feed the funny monkey in my brain, my anxiety working as a conduit. I didn't envy the couple's fate, but I envied the passion Rebecca seemed to possess for I haven't been very lucky at love. My talent never quite equaled my aspirations, but that didn't mean I was ready for a courtship with a ghost. Had the long-dead Rebecca, still hungering from her loss, returned for me? Could the extraordinary gift of *sight* have somehow enabled her return when the situation was right?

At dusk and beyond, a strange mix of fear and curiosity held me to this place. I began to nurture my fears like an appetite until it had grown into something bloated and undying. In the hallway, a grandfather clock continued to tick away the passing moments with mechanical precision while all else seemed distorted. I must have been attempting to give my house the characteristics of the one I had seen in the photograph. Better than to believe the house was truly organic, twisting and turning into shapes from the ancient past.

In the evenings I had become a receptacle of fear, starting at the slightest sound, glancing constantly into dark corners. Something seen, then unseen. There, then not there. As I sat at my desk trying to distract myself with paperwork of some sort, a gust of wind rattled the windowpanes. The walls groaned. Every creak sounded like a footstep. My eyes traveled the room. I could almost hear a shuffling at the front door and see it cant slightly off plum before slowly opening. Rebecca would stand at the threshold. If I closed my eyes for a moment, all would be well, like the rational ticking of the clock that now sounded a bit like nails pounding into the lid of a coffin. But still, I wondered if a preordained dance summoned by a historical choreography kept me tied to a power that asserted itself from beyond the grave.

Then came the evening of actual contact.

Thunder sounded like a cannon volley and rattled the rafters. Razorblades of lightening slashed into my bedroom, but it wasn't the sound and fury that bothered me most. Wind was banging the gate where Rebecca first appeared. A loose vine slapped against a drain pipe. The ground seemed to be trembling below me and the sky splitting overhead. I felt like a kid in a dark house on Halloween. I didn't dare to look out of the window for I feared the sight of something standing in the yard beside the shrubs, something near the house, or even peering through the window.

The night pressed down on me like a pile of blankets. I thought about how alone I was, how far my world had detached from one of the pleasant dreams. The patter of rain that might have lulled me to sleep failed to follow. I eventually succumbed to the lateness of the hour, but on a storm filled night, the boundary between dreams and reality can be porous. In a dream, cold lips brushed against my cheek and forehead. I gasped and opened my eyes. I was alone in a room that was as cold as the touch had been. I was convinced Rebecca was about to take dramatic action for at the time of the most recent sighting, she was at the porch steps, holding the cloth bag open with clawed hands.

My fear was no longer abstract. It now had weight and substance. I could feel it with every nerve ending in my body. The next evening, the sun disappeared as if running away from the world, taking with it the light that didn't want to be left behind. There was heaviness to the air that had nothing to do with the weather, a charged density. Did I dare close my eyes? I tried to find some semblance of rest while the pounding of my heart seemed audible. I found myself in that dim zone between sleep and wakefulness. I sensed something extraordinary was about to happen. If I fell asleep, would I feel a hand on my shoulder? The stillness of the house pressed around me. It was like the moment of silence that precedes a scream. Could this whole business conclude with my sanity slipping away? The fabric of my life was tearing apart like rotted silk and I seemed powerless to stop it. The frightening word "possession" entered my mind again. I was neither a drinker nor a druggie, but this was one time I believed a drink or a hit would have calmed me. There existed unresolved information the living might inherit from the departed as I continued on a mind-bending ride to the edge of madness.

A series of sounds followed; glass cracking, furniture moving slightly, noises starting in one room and moving to another. But the worst of all was the faint odor of decay. Was any of this real or just phantoms inside my head?

Then a subtler sound, a creak in a floorboard; Rebecca was near. Was she lingering in the darkness by choice or by necessity? I awaited the sound of hinges squeaking or the click of a latch, assuming objects such as these were a hindrance. Or might it be a soft knock on the door to be followed by a presence looming up in the night like some fearful monster, casting a long shadow in the dimness of the moonlit room, if she *could* cast a shadow. And when it came, would I feel the coldness of dead lips on my flesh, or something more spectacular like clawed fingertips hooking into my flesh and pulling me into some unimaginable place? Would it be like a jolt from an electrical wire when she revealed the contents of her bag? I shoved a corner of my quilt into my mouth to keep from screaming.

As the night quieted, I believed I could actually hear the house breathe. In the dimness of the shadowed bedroom, I felt the air around me compress. If I'd entered Rebecca's coffin, the atmosphere couldn't have been more oppressive. I was a puppet with Rebecca pulling the strings. Was my fate to be determined by a woman who was both above the earth as well as below it? What could I do but lay still in the gloom, listening and hoping the horror would pass while my heart thudded behind the wall of my chest. Could I ever sleep again without taking action, before something tore loose inside of me that could never be repaired? I'd developed the kind of fear you feel when a voice inside you whispers evil is not only real, but nothing can save you from it. I had become like an addict who fears dreams and reality, a slave to my perceptions.

My trusty clock stopped ticking so abruptly that its silence sliced through the room like a scythe. I knew I was irretrievably slipping into the abyss. If I succumbed to the inner darkness that beckoned me, all would be lost. It was at that moment when a strange notion engulfed me, one that couldn't be banished. I wanted no more nights forfeited to the unknown. There was no remedy for this kind of fear except action. I decided what I must do.

◊ ◊ ◊ ◊

A week has passed since I waited for that knock or a kiss, or something far worse. And here I remain in this little burg a century and a half after Rebecca was laid to an uneasy rest, the most recent in a long line of caretakers on land sold or rented many times over. But I am no longer considering giving up my domicile in the quaint town of Albion, Illinois. Friends and acquaintances in Chicago will have to wait until my mission is complete. The house seems to have righted itself, its angular verticality restored. The quandary over what would satisfy Rebecca has been resolved in part. Even though the situation isn't perfect, it appears that acquiring both me and the house has soothed the wandering wraith.

Before she had the opportunity to take control in whatever manner she chose with her tapestry bag and gnarled hands, I decided to remove the curtain of fear before me by paying another visit to the cemetery under the veil of darkness. My nocturnal labors took less time than I would have thought because rain had softened the ground part way. Under a moon emerging from behind clouds like a big spying eye, I began to dig. In the gloom, the gravestones had become horizontal slats of shadow. I halfway expected to see Rebecca's spectral presence standing next to one of the tombstones observing my progress. The only sounds were that of a slight breeze and my labored breathing from the physical exertion I was unaccustomed to. The only time I wavered in my task was when my head disappeared beneath the ground's surface and I could no longer watch for…whatever, as a cold moisture oozed up from the soil, seeping into my garments like a wet vapor. I wondered where the expression *six feet under* came from for I could swear I'd passed that depth a foot ago. Maybe those who buried Rebecca thought she needed an extra few feet considering her unique circumstance. It wasn't until the fresh pile of dirt made the hole seem another two feet deep when I finally heard the sound of my shovel splinter rotted wood. I worked quicker until the sought-after item was found. I crossed myself in spite of my heretofore agnosticism, just in case I had committed a sin against either the earth or spirits, or both.

I scraped away as much dirt as I could for fear the lid would totally collapse under my weight and make a mess of whatever was left of Rebecca. I then knocked the corroded lock loose and opened the lid on creaky hinges that broke off after a mere foot of stress. Pushing the lid aside, I beheld what was left of Mrs. Mason, which wasn't much. A gag reflex kicked in as I looked upon the fleshless, toothy grin and the hollow eye-sockets. Her apparition had certainly been more recognizable than her remains. Nature's cleanup had performed its duty and fed on this death long ago. Her coffin and clothes had deteriorated to the point of near nonexistence. Her bones would have fallen apart if not for the few scraps of leathery skin, remnants as brown and dry as a chamois. My imaginings about claw-like hands were dispelled, at least for the time being, now that her body was free to accompany her spirit.

For transport, I carefully wrapped her remains in a tarpaulin and tried to repair the disturbed earth from which one of its own had been taken. I was a few aches beyond bone tired, but my mind was racing. The hardest part was the return trip with Rebecca's remains bumping around on the backseat of my car. "If I've overstepped my bounds by taking you, Rebecca, let the woman I've been seeing take the breath out of me for daring to help," I babbled like a confused man trying to justify what I'd just done. In the gray ghost of the approaching dawn, I couldn't bear to look in the rearview mirror due to the lingering fear she might toss aside the canvas shroud and attempt to physically complete whatever her mission might have been. I had seen it happen in too many movies.

I realized few things in my life would ever be the same after that night in the graveyard. I had reached a border that would separate the future from everything that had gone before. My soul would never again belong to me alone. With my help, Rebecca journeyed beyond the veil of death and into my living room, earthbound again in body, of sorts. It's not as if she can have the joy of life, but she can at least sit near a window and survey the land she and Yardley shared. With a little ingenuity using wire and superglue, she hangs together pretty well, and I found her a dress at Goodwill for modesty's sake. Now I can talk to her every day about this, that, or the other. That is something at least—having the company of a man who is all in one piece.

Could she be grieving still, or do all one-hundred and fifty year old corpses possess the same mournful, downcast countenance? I whistle a tune now and then thinking Rebecca might appreciate music. Once, while in another room, I thought I heard her bones clacking around as if dancing. I ran in expecting to see the dress whirling about, but she was back at the window, Yardley's head securely between her bony fingers.

Oh yes, Yardley's head. It had been buried with her in a metal box, leaving it in somewhat better condition than she. He has more hair than she. Even though his toothy leer can be offsetting, it seems only right it should rest in Rebecca's lap after she found the supernatural means to retrieve it.

If the Mason's remains should be discovered within the confines of our home, it will surely add a fresh chapter to the tale of restless spirits and give credence to the theory that the past, or those that occupy it, is never completely dead.

Seek no longer the beloved.

The words ring hollow because the freeing of her earthly remains from the grave has not concluded Rebecca's search. The words "until death do us part" must not always apply. I am convinced she is beckoning for assistance in finding the rest of Yardley. Unless there was a happy, heavenly reunion after death, which apparently wasn't the case for Rebecca, what must it be like to spend eternity with only part of a loved one? I believe she wants Yardley to join her in a final dance to erase the horror of his demise at the hands of warring brutes. Although her eye sockets are as vacant as a parking lot after closing hours, I believe she can see. At times, I feel I could open the dress she's wearing and witness the beating of her heart.

An image of an old kitchen preceding the one where I now stand sometimes overwhelms me. A woman in a bell-shaped skirt stands over a wood stove, the smell of bacon frying and chicory coffee brewing fills my nostrils. Rebecca, preparing breakfast for... The vision and the aromas vanish as nearly as soon as they arrive. Now that I have permitted her access to the house, I anticipate continuing incidents until our destinies become clear.

Somewhere I read it wasn't true that the insane thought themselves sane. They often do not fight their affliction because there are pleasures and beauty in madness. One thing for sure, I have developed new sensitivities. There have been sweet justifications in my actions. The clock still ticks away slices of time, but real time only matters to flesh and blood. Eventually, I will be informed how this reunion is to play out because I believe the cadaver of Rebecca is very nearly ready to speak to me.

AUTHOR BIOGRAPHIES

Stuart Conover

Stuart Conover is a father, husband, blogger, published author, geek, entrepreneur, and horror fanatic. He lives in the Chicagoland area and when not delving into the land of horror, comics, and science fiction he spends his days working in IT and his nights with his family. Passionate about writing you can find his work in a variety of outlets and books. When does he sleep you may ask? No one is sure that he does!

Website: www.StuartConover.com

Eli Constant

Eli Constant is a genre-jumping detail junkie, obsessed with the nature of humanity. She believes that there is beauty at the core of most everything, but that truly unredeemable characters create the best stories. Eli is the author of *Dead Trees*, *Dead Trees 2*, *Mastic*, *DRAG.N*, and is a contributor to several current and upcoming anthologies. Among these is: *Let's Scare Cancer to Death* (MayDecember Publications), a charity anthology providing 100% of proceeds to the **V Foundation**. While completing coursework at USC-L, Columbia College, TAMU-CC, and George Mason University, Eli enjoyed a varied course load, but finally settled on Biology and focused on a career in lab research. She spent time in Texas at Flour Bluff Shrimp Mariculture Lab and also spent time at NIH participating in an Animal Research Program in the Infectious Disease Dept. It took two years working in Histology/Pathology for her to realize she wanted to be a writer.

Eli lives in Virginia with her husband Damion, their two children (with their third on the way), and her rescue hound. Find out more: www.eliconstant.com and keep posted on upcoming publications.

ERIC I. DEAN

Eric Dean lives and works in Tulsa, OK. He has a degree in English from Oklahoma State University, and spends his time writing (www.ericwrites.com) and crafting (www.thepostapoc.com, or facebook.com/ thepostapoc). You can also follow him on Twitter @thepostapoc. His least favorite thing to write is a third-person bio.

FRANK J. EDLER

Frank J. Edler resides in New Jersey where he attempts to write. His first short story collection, *Scared Silly,* is available in eBook and paperback from all major online retailers. His stories can also be found in *Still Dying 2, Strange Versus Lovecraft* and *Strange Fucking Stories* anthologies. His writing spans Horror to Bizzaro and points in between. He is co-host of the wildly popular podcast *Books, Beer and Bullshit.* His podcasting antics can be heard at booksbeerbullshit.podbean.com or the companion blog booksbeerblogshit.blogspot.com. Read his own blog at FrankJEdler.Blogspot.Com

Look for Frank's first full length novel, *Brats In Hell,* late 2014/early 2015.

A. LOPEZ JR.

Born and raised in Texas and now living in Arizona, I began writing seriously in 2009.

I published my first work *Purgatory – 13 Tales of the Macabre* in 2011, and soon after, *Floor Four* – A Novella of Horror. I am currently writing the *Night Dreams* Series (1-3 available) with more episodes to be released every couple of months. My column "Ask AJ" appears in the *All Authors Magazine,* and I have short stories published at Dark River

Press and *The Sirens Call eZine Issue #14*. I feel horror stories should be read at night, in a dark room, with the soft glow of a reading light being your only friend and the only barrier between you and that dark corner of the room; the one you keep glancing at every time you hear a strange noise. In that setting, your mind will let your senses take over. Every sound will be magnified, and every shadow will move, as you absorb each word delivered to your mind's eye. That is the best way to enjoy a story of horror, in my opinion. Just food for thought.

Please visit me at: alopezjr.com and join THE PROJECT, my free newsletter or follow me on Twitter @acehilink

P. DAVID PUFFINBURGER

When I was a child doing farm work my mind would wonder and make up stories, but I never wrote them down. After high school I worked as an electrician until I joined the Army serving from 2000-2003. I saw and learned a lot in those years. I am a disabled veteran so I have plenty of time to write. My lap top and thumb drives are full stories. I have several novels that could be turned to a series but they are still sitting on the shelf, so to speak. If anyone wants to contact me please feel to do so on Facebook.

My top five stories I have written are *Death Infection* (zombie story), *Dog the Boy* (a tutored young boy is helped by a demon), *Dust* (the world is covered in volcanic ash), *Death Infection 203* (sequel to *Death Infection*), *Flint the Grassman Killer* (a revolution war veteran is hired to find the Ohio Grassman) I have been published by Armand Rosamilia's *Undead Tales*, "Horror Carnival" and "Creature Feature" by Open Casket Press

HERIKA R. RAYMER

Herika R. Raymer grew up consuming books—first by eating them, later by reading them. Her mother taught her the value of focus and hard work while her father encouraged her love literature and art; so she has been writing and doodling off and on for over 30 years. After much encouragement, Mrs. Raymer finally published a few short stories and has developed a taste for it. She continues to send submissions, sometimes with success, and currently has a collection of stories in the works. She was the Assistant Editor for a science fiction magazine and Lead Editor for a horror magazine, so has a healthy respect for proofing and editing. A participant of the voluntary writer/artist/musician cooperative known as Imagicopter, Herika R. Raymer is married with two children and a dog in West Tennessee, USA.

Website: herikarraymer.webs.com

Stories available:

"Dook" in *Hero's Best Friend* from Seventh Star Press

"Immortality" in *Ink Monkey Magazine-Issue 5* from Ink Monkey Press

"Clash"/"Believe" in Mytherium: Tales of Mythical and Magical Creatures from Indigo Publishing

"Little of Stature, Big of Daring" in *Dragons Composed* from Dark Oak Press/Kerlak Publishing

CLAIRE C. RILEY

Claire C. Riley is a #1 Best Selling British Horror writer.

Her work is best described as the modernization of classic, old-school horror. She fuses multi-genre elements to develop storylines that pay homage to cult-classics while still feeling fresh and cutting-edge. She writes characters that are realistic, and kills them without mercy.

Claire lives in the UK with her husband, three daughters, and one scruffy dog.

Odium. The Dead Saga is a top *#100 dystopian* selling book on Amazon.com for 2013, 'Indie book of the day' winner December 2013 and 'Indie Author Land 50 best self-published books worth reading 2013/14'

Limerence featured book in the 'Guardian newspaper for best Indie novel 2013' and is currently a finalist for the eFestival of Words 'best novel' category.

Odium II The Dead Saga is a *#1 Best Selling British Horror* book.

She is also a very proud contributor to the *Let's Scare Cancer to Death* charity anthology.

Visit Claire C. Riley at her website:
www.clairecriley.com

ARMAND ROSAMILIA

Armand Rosamilia is a New Jersey boy currently living in sunny Florida, where he exacts revenge on his enemies and neighbors alike by writing them into his *Dying Days* zombie series. And not in good ways. He has over 120 releases to date, with more coming. He is also a radio and internet DJ and runs *Arm Cast: Dead Sexy Horror Podcast*, with interviews from the best authors, etc. in horror. He loves talking in third person. He can be reached at armandrosamilia.com and armandrosamilia@gmail.com if you want to chat.

JAY SEATE

No matter how Mr. Seate starts a story, it inevitably turns to the macabre. It may be told with hard core realism or erotic humor, but it gets his pulse racing enough to pull his corpse from the grave to write something new. He is especially keen on stories that transcend genre pigeonholing. His stories and memoirs appear in numerous magazines, newspapers, anthologies and webzines.

Recent ones can be found at:

www.melange-books.com/authors/jtroyseate/jtroyseate.html museituppublishing.com for those who like their tales intertwined with the paranormal.

See it all at www.troyseateauthor.webs.com

JULIANNE SNOW

Julianne Snow is the author of the *Days with the Undead* series and *Glimpses of the Undead*. She is the founder of Zombieholics Anonymous and the Publicist at Sirens Call Publications. Writing in the realms of speculative fiction, Julianne has roots that go deep into horror and is a member of the Horror Writers Association. With pieces of short fiction in various publications, Julianne always has a few surprises up her sleeves. Be sure to check out *The Carnival 13*, a collaborative round-robin novella for charity which she contributed to and helped to spearhead which was released in October 2013.

Julianne Snow's blogs:
Days With The Undead (dayswiththeundead.com),
The FlipSide of Julianne
(theflipsideofjulianne.wordpress.com),
Zombieholics Anonymous (zombieholicsanonymous.com)

DJ TYRER

DJ Tyrer has worked in education and public relations and is the person behind *Atlantean Publishing* and has been widely published in anthologies and magazines in the UK, USA and elsewhere, most recently in *Steampunk Cthulhu* (Chaosium), *Tales of the Dark Arts* (Hazardous Press), *Cosmic*

Horror (Dark Hall Press), *Serial Killers Quattuor* (JWK Fiction), and *Fossil Lake* (Sabledrake Enterprises), and, in addition, has two novellas available on the Kindle, *The Yellow House* (Dynatox Ministries) and *Acting Strangely* (Jazzclaw Publishing).

DJ Tyrer's website is at djtyrer.blogspot.co.uk

DELLA WEST

Della West lives in Vicksburg, Mississippi and enjoys writing in a number of different genres. Horror, Paranormal, Fantasy and Cowboy Poetry. She is currently working on two novels set in World War II. Other published works include and can be found in the following anthologies. "Battle for Vicksburg" *Southern Haunts 2: Devils in the Darkness.* "Find Myself a Cowboy" *Unbridled Volume One*, and "The Apartment House" in the upcoming *Southern Haunts 3.*

If you would like to contact Della, email her at DellaWestAuthor@yahoo.com

ABOUT THE EDITOR

Jerry Benns started writing when he was quite young. However, he began seriously writing in 2010 by launching his blog, TripThroughMyMind.com. Since then, he has expanded the site to include interviews with authors, book reviews, and sections to encourage building the writing community. Jerry's deep-seated enjoyment of reading and writing now has him embarking on the exciting journey of publishing by launching Charon Coin Press.

In 2014, after becoming the editor for the State of Horror anthology series, Jerry pursued the opportunity to purchase the series, and others, in order to release them under his new publishing company, Charon Coin Press. Jerry brings his experience from his previous marketing/branding company, as well 15 years of experience as a networker and project manager to Charon Coin Press.

Jerry continues to write short stories and his blog, in addition to working on an urban fantasy series. He also looks for ways to share the love of reading and books to the next generation.

◇

Charon Coin Press

◇

◇

Chosen Coin Press

◇

◇

Charon Coin Press

◇

Charon Coin Press